PUBLISHER'S NOTE

This is the seventh volume of Charlie Small's amazing journal. A toothless old docker found it whilst unloading a ship at the port of London town. A heavy spice barrel slipped from his hands and smashed wide open, spilling a pile of strong-smelling powder across the quayside. Sticking out of the powder was a battered notebook.

The astonished docker flicked through the pages; they told the most incredible tales of derring-do, and he knew he'd discovered a rare Charlie Small journal. He sent it straight off to us, and now everyone can share Charlie's latest and greatest adventures!

There must be other notebooks to find, so keep your eyes peeled. If you do come across a curious-looking diary, or see an eight-year-old boy wearing a jet-powered rucksack, please let us know at the website: www.charliesmall.co.uk

Guess who I bump into

Uh!

THE AMAZING ADVENTURES OF CHARLIE SMALL (400)

Notebook 7

The Mummy's Tomb

Danger, danger!

Watch out for smoke demons Aaargh!

RED FOX

NAME: Charlie Small

ADDRESS: Jakeman's Factory

AGE: 400 - give or take a few years

MOBILE: 0771312

SCHOOL: St Beckham's - although I've been on holiday for four hundred years. Brilliant

THINGS I LIKE:
Cutlass fighting; Braemar; Jenny and Granny Green; Tom, Eliza and Ma Baldwin; Jakeman and Philly; Thrak!

THINGS I HATE: Joseph Craik (my arch enemy); electric horned eels; The Potentate of Mayazapan; skeletal swordsmen; the menagerie mincing machine

CHARLIE SMALL: THE MUMMY'S TOMB
A RED FOX BOOK 978 1 782 95328 9

First published in Great Britain by David Fickling Books,
(when an imprint of Random House Children's Publishers UK
A Random House Group Company)

This Red Fox edition published 2014

5 7 9 10 8 6 4

**Penguin Random House is committed to a sustainable future for
our business, our readers and our planet. This book is made from
Forest Stewardship Council® certified paper.**

Printed and bound in Great Britain by Clays Ltd, St Ives plc

Set in 15/17pt Garamond MT

Red Fox Books are published by Random House Children's Publishers UK,
61–63 Uxbridge Road, London W5 5SA

www.randomhousechildrens.co.uk
www.totallyrandombooks.co.uk
www.randomhouse.co.uk

Addresses for companies within The Random House Group Limited can be found at: www.
randomhouse.co.uk/offices.htm

THE RANDOM HOUSE GROUP Limited Reg. No. 954009

A CIP catalogue record for this book is available from the British Library.

If you find this book, **PLEASE** look after it. This is the only true account of my remarkable adventures.

My name is Charlie Small and I am four hundred years old, maybe even more. But in all those long years I have never grown up. Something happened when I was eight years old, something I can't begin to understand. I went on a journey... and I'm still trying to find my way home. Now, although I've been nearly frazzled by a horned electric eel, attacked by sword-wielding skeletons and chased by a mob of armed chimps, I still look like any eight-year-old boy you might pass in the street.

I've been nearly suffocated by a smoke demon and rescued by a mythical winged panther. You may think this sounds fantastic, you could think it's a lie. But you would be wrong, because **EVERYTHING IN THIS BOOK IS TRUE.** Believe this single fact and you can share the most incredible journey ever experienced.

Charlie Small

The world went black!

Body Snatchers!

'Hey! What's going on?' I yelled.

Suddenly, my world was plunged into darkness. Raising my hands, I felt coarse, scratchy material surrounding me. Someone had thrust a sack over my head!

'Got him!' a man's voice growled. 'Let's take him down to the docks!'

'No!' I yelled in a real panic. 'I'm supposed to be going to Jakeman's.'

'Well, you're not,' said another man's voice. 'You're comin' with us, whether you like it or not.'

'Let me go, you goons!' I cried and, although I couldn't see a thing, I kicked out like a bad-tempered donkey.

'Ouch! Keep still, you little pest,' snarled the first voice again. 'Stop strugglin' or we'll bop you on the 'ead.'

I yelled in frustration. This was terrible! Just when everything had been going so well . . .

A few days earlier, I had managed to rescue the reindeer herder, Mamuk, from the bloodthirsty brigands of Frostbite Pass; he had taken me zooming across a wintery sky on a magical sleigh ride and dropped me off on a grassy hilltop overlooking a wide river valley.

Below me was a town, its narrow streets busy with people whose shouts and laughter carried up to me through the clear, still air. Further along, at the river mouth, stood some decrepit docks where a tangle of masts and rigging poked above sagging warehouses.

Then, peering across the valley through my powerful telescope, I had spied my pal Jakeman's fabulous factory. AT LAST! I'd been trying to find this place for ages: Jakeman's incredible inventions and miraculous machines had helped me out of countless sticky situations on my travels. All I needed to do was cross the valley, climb the headland to the factory and he would surely invent something to send me home.

But everything went wrong! As soon as I set out on the winding track that led across the valley, these boneheads bunged a sack over my head. Now they were manhandling me along the stony path, pushing and shoving and growling at me to keep quiet. I tried to fire up my new jet-powered rucksack but the thugs had my arms clamped to my side and I couldn't reach the buttons. I kicked out again.

'Right, that's it, I've had enough!' said one of the men.

'You've been warned,' muttered the other, and they lifted me up and carried me between them like a sack of potatoes. I continued to struggle but it was no good; the brutes were much too strong.

Before long I sensed we were nearing the docks. The tweeting of thrushes and blackbirds gave way to the harsh cry of seagulls, and the smell of grass was replaced with the salty tang of sea air. What did these mysterious body-snatchers want with me?

A Den of Thieves

All of a sudden the sack was yanked from my head and I found myself staring at two of the roughest, toughest-looking men I had ever seen. They were broad-shouldered, thick-necked, shaven-headed brutes dressed in the garb of itinerant seafarers.

We were standing in a narrow alleyway that ran between a huddle of tall, sea-battered and decaying buildings. Ahead, the alley opened onto the dockside where I could hear the shouts and cries of sailors loading ships. Seeing a chance of escape, I went for the launch button of my jetpack rucksack, but one of the men was too quick. His hand

closed around my wrist, pulling it away from the switch.

'Now, now,' he said, yanking the pack from my back, 'I'll look after this for a while if you don't mind.'

'What do you want with me?' I cried. 'Give me back my explorer's kit!'

'Calm down, boy! You can have it back later. Just do as we say and everything'll be fine,' he said, wagging a short, fat finger in my face. 'Ain't that right, Perce?'

'That's right, Syd,' said the other man. 'We ain't gonna hurt you, boy – unless you make it necessary. Now, we've gotta go through the Black Swan, but we can't take you in a busy pub with this sack over yer 'ead.'

'Why not, are you worried someone might try to rescue me, you great bullies?' I said, kicking out at their ankles again.

Syd laughed and shook me by the shoulder. 'The beer-swillin' buccaneers of the Black Swan, rescue you? You must be jokin'! They're the biggest bunch of low-down dogs you'll ever meet. No, they won't try and rescue you, but they might try and slit yer gizzard. They *hate* strangers. They *loathe* outsiders. Pretend you're pals with us, Charlie, and you just might survive!'

With a hoarse chuckle, he pushed me into the low, dark entrance of the Black Swan Inn. I stepped into a cacophony of roaring and laughing and singing.

My captors pushed me through the crowds of people. There was an overwhelming smell of stale beer and old sweaty clothes, and a thousand hostile eyes were directed towards me.

'Stranger in our midst!' shouted a toothless old man, thrusting his leering face into mine. *Phwoar!* His breath stank of strong, spicy rum and I reeled back in shock.

'Leave the boy be,' said Syd. 'He's with us.'

'And what do you want wiv a sprat like that? Maybe he's got a purse worth slicin' open,' sneered the

The stinky toothless old man!

rum-soaked reprobate, and he slid out a small dagger from the folds of his filthy coat. Perce grabbed his skinny wrist, twisting it until the blade clattered to the floor.

'We said, leave him be,' said Perce menacingly.

'Don't be like that, Perce,' squealed the old soak, rubbing his wrist. 'I was only havin' a bit o' fun; why don't you stay and 'ave a drop of the 'ard stuff?'

'We 'aven't got time to waste drinkin' with the likes o' you, Jimmy Jones,' said Perce. The old man cursed as Syd and Perce shoved past him and propelled me deeper into the crowd. Weaving through the throng was an enormously fat man carrying a tray piled with tankards and goblets, pies and sizzling chops.

'*He's* been askin' for yer,' the man said to Syd with a nod of his head towards the rear of the room. 'Who's your young friend?'

'Just someone Mr Twitch has been expectin',' said Syd with a grin. 'And I suppose his lordship will be wantin' his meal soon. Is it ready?'

'Ready and waitin',' said the enormous landlord. 'He can have it whenever he wants.'

Who on earth is this Twitch fellow they're on about? I wondered. He must be their

The landlord of the Black Swan

boss – and it was clear he was expecting me. I pictured the thugs' boss as a huge, powerfully-built man, bulging with muscles and covered in scars, and I went weak at the knees. *Yikes!*

How wrong could I be!

11

Bony elbows cracked against my face and my feet were stamped on by a multitude of hobnail boots as I pressed through the rollicking horde, but no one else took any notice of me. Then, above the din, I heard some voices singing a familiar song:

We were poor little wives of black-hearted pirates,
Who left us at home, playing at mum,
But now we've become the scourge of the oceans,
So watch your backs and pass me the rum.

Rum, rum (fresh, slimy gizzards)
Rum, rum (saltwater scum)
Rum, rum (don't spit in the wind, girls)
Rum, rum, just pass me the rum.

How strange! It was the song Captain Cut-throat and her crew used to sing aboard the *Betty Mae* when I was the most wanted pirate on the wide Pangaean ocean! Did that mean my old shipmates were in port? I was just about to cry for help when I remembered the last time I had seen the Perfumed Pirates of Perfidy. They had been firing round after round of musket shot at me as I escaped in my homemade

(See my Journal Pirate galleon)

barrel-boat. They called me a sneaking traitor and a dirty deserter and said they would skin me alive if they ever saw me again – maybe they weren't the right people to help!

But before I could decide whether to call out or not, Perce unlatched a worm-eaten door at the back of the pub and I was shoved outside into a courtyard. We crossed the yard to a long, tall building on the opposite side. The ground floor was lined with a row of barred windows and wide sliding doors, all heavily padlocked.

'What *is* this place?' I asked, but my two captors didn't reply. They led me to the nearest corner of the building where there was another smaller door, which Syd unlocked with a large key and then pushed open to reveal a steep flight of steps.

'Follow me,' he growled, and with Perce taking up the rear, I nervously followed him up the dark staircase into a room that stretched the entire length of the building. I had no idea what to expect, but in my mind's eye and with knees trembling, I pictured this vicious, mean and dastardly gang leader.

Shafts of sunlight, swirling with dust, streamed through a line of grubby windows as

I was marched forward; casks and boxes were piled high against the walls; ropes hanging from block and tackle sets snaked down from the ceiling above and disappeared through hatches in the floor. The air was filled with the pungent smells of strange spices, tobaccos and tar. Then, in the gloom, I spied Syd and Percy's feared leader.

Lounging on an ornate sofa, was a skinny man dressed in a scarlet coat, a fancy, frilled shirt and knee-length breeches.

My name is Tristram Twitch

One of his smooth, pink cheeks was decorated with a beauty spot and he held a lace handkerchief to his long, elegant nose. He looked a right sissy!

'Oh, hurrah! Sydenham! Percy! Any luck?' he cried out in a silly high voice.

'Got 'im, sir,' said Syd and shoved me forward.

'Well done! Do come here, Charlie – it is Charlie Small, I presume?' he twittered. 'I'd hate to think we'd got the wrong boy again!'

This chap looks about as dangerous as a french poodle! I thought, and my courage returned. What on earth had I been worried about?

'Oh, it's 'im all right, sir. And a right wriggler and kicker he is too!' said Syd, rubbing his bruised shins.

'Who are you and what do you want?' I demanded. I'd had just about enough of being pushed around!

Tristram Twitch ← ooh lala!

'Oh, don't be like that, Charlie!' said the man in

15

his soft, sing-song voice. He languidly got to his feet and glided lazily over to a long table that was set out for dinner. It was as if the exertion of these few steps was enough to wear him out and he collapsed into a tall-backed chair with a sigh.

'My name is Tristram Twitch and I mean you no harm, my dear Charlie. Really! As long as you decide to help me, of course! Come and have something to eat and I will explain everything.'

I didn't like the sound of this, even coming from such a dandified drip.

'No way. I'm not going to eat with someone who's just kidnapped me!' I protested. But then, soon after Syd had pulled a bell cord that hung at the side of the room, the huge man from the pub came puffing up the stairs followed by half a dozen waiters. They were all carrying trays laden with the most delicious smelling food. I hadn't eaten anything all day, and despite myself my tummy rumbled with hunger.

'Well, perhaps just a bite,' I mumbled and sat down at the table.

'That's more like it, Charlie,' smiled Tristram, spooning a goggle-eyed fish's head onto my plate. 'Try a coddled cod's head, and I'll explain my predicament.'

As the landlord and the waiters left, Syd and Perce sat down with us, grinning stupidly. Syd

A coddled cod head

didn't wait to be served, but grabbed a cod's head in his fist and pushed the whole thing into his mouth. With a slurping, slobbering noise he sucked the head of all its flesh and spat the skull out onto his plate. Then, with his tongue, he pushed the fish's grey eyes between his teeth and bit down. They popped like bubble wrap and he licked the eye jelly from his lips with relish. Ugh – disgusting!

'Manners, Sydenham,' said Twitch with a sigh, popping a flake of fish into his mouth and then dabbing his lips with a giant linen serviette. 'We have guests.'

'Pardon me,' apologized Syd with a belch.

As I tucked into my cod's head and followed it up with barbequed whale blubber, jellyfish trifle and tankards of foaming squid-ink ale, my debonair kidnapper told me what he wanted me for. And the more I heard, the less I liked the sound of what he was saying . . .

The Three TERRIBLE Tasks!

He finished a mouthful and dabbed at his mouth with his lace handkerchief. 'As I said, Charlie, my name is Tristram Twitch and I'm a gentleman with *great* expectations. But I desperately need your help, Charlie – and Jakeman said you were *just* the boy for the job.'

'You're a friend of Jakeman's?' I cried, with my mouth full of chewy blubber. If this twit knew Jakeman, perhaps I still had a chance of meeting up with the friendly inventor and getting home. 'Why didn't you just say so in the first place, instead of bunging a sack over my head and dragging me here against my will?'

'Good point, Charlie. But I wouldn't say I was a friend of Jakeman's exactly,' drawled Twitch with a sneaky look on his chinless face. 'Let me explain from the start. I am engaged to marry the daughter of Lord Larouche – a sweet girl, very rich and absolutely *mad* about me. Isn't that right, boys?'

'Oh yeah! She's absolutely loaded!' grinned Syd moronically and Perce gave a snort.

'Unfortunately Aveline is rather spoiled,' continued Tristram Twitch. 'And before we marry she wants me to *prove* my devotion to her – dear, sweet thing that she is!'

'Big deal! What's that got to do with me?' I asked.

'Well, Aveline has set me three tasks; I have to get her some priceless presents before our wedding can go ahead. She wants a pearl from the giant oyster beds of Broomania, a diamond tiara from the head of the mummified Princess of Purh, and she wants a solid gold spine plucked from the back of the world's last surviving golden porcupine. He is kept in a fantastic zoo on the island of Mayazapan. They aren't easy tasks, by any stretch of the imagination – but they shouldn't be too much trouble for an intrepid adventurer like *you*, Charlie!'

'Me!' I exclaimed.

'Exactly! You see, I'm not a very adventurous fellow, and the idea of sailing across the wild ocean fills me with dread – even with these two great ugly brutes to guard me.'

'Great ugly brutes?' chorused Syd and Perce, looking hurt.

'But, I do love my Aveline dearly,' said Twitch, ignoring his minders. 'And if I don't get her these trinkets I won't get my hands on her fortune, er, I mean I won't be able to marry my beloved. I bravely decided I *must* at least try to get her pressies, so I went to see Jakeman the famous inventor, to kit myself out for the dangerous expedition and he told me all about you, Charlie Small, adventurer extraordinaire!

'That immediately got my old brain working,' Twitch continued, tapping a forefinger against his head as he gulped down the last of his squid-ink ale. 'If this chap Charlie Small is such a great adventurer, I thought, why shouldn't *he* go in my place? Jakeman said he was hoping you'd turn up pronto, so I sent Syd and Percy to keep a look out for you. You're the sixth lad they've brought back, but finally we've got the right one. Of course, Aveline will never know it was you that went on the great adventure, and when I present her with her gifts, she'll think I'm the bravest hero in the world!'

What? 'Well, I'm sorry to disappoint you, Mr

Twitch, but there's no *way* I'm going off on a completely unnecessary adventure. It might be dangerous and I wouldn't even know where to start looking for your presents. I'm going home. Jakeman has already told me he can help get me there. So, no deal, I'm afraid.'

'Ah!' said Twitch with a smirk. 'You don't understand, my young friend; if you *don't* do as I ask, the results will be catastrophic – and you won't be going anywhere! Syd, Percy; it's time to show Charlie the special contraption we've rigged up. That should change his mind. I would show you myself, but I'm feeling absolutely exhausted.'

I Change My Mind!

How come Twitch is so sure I'll help him? I wondered, as Syd and Perce marched me to the end of the room. I didn't have to wait long to find out.

I was led past boxes marked with ornate stamps, secreting exotic and mysterious smells, to where a wooden flight of stairs led us up to another long room. I was taken to where a heavy rope disappeared through an open hatchway in the floor.

'See that?' asked Syd, pointing. A heavy sack was tied to the end of the rope in a small, dark storeroom below our feet.

'Yes,' I said, confused.

'Now look,' said Syd and pointed up to where the rope passed around a pulley wheel attached to a beam above our head. I followed him as he traced the rope with his forefinger, to where it passed through an aperture above an open loading door. The rope passed around another wheel on a gantry outside and dropped from sight.

'Go on, take a look,' he said and I stepped out onto a rickety wooden platform. Wow! It was really high and I felt a little queasy as my gaze followed the rope down to where a king-sized lobster pot was tied to the other end. It dangled about twelve metres above the oil-slicked surface of an enclosed, water-filled pit – and in it was my friend, Jakeman! He

Jakeman looked very miserable

was dressed in a pair of oily overalls, looking thoroughly miserable and his huge, peppery-brown moustache drooped forlornly.

'Jakeman!' I called out.

'Charlie, is that you?' cried my old friend, but before I could say any more, Syd dragged me back inside the warehouse and slammed the hoist doorway closed.

'That's enough chatter,' he snarled.

'What are you doing?' I stammered. 'Why is Jakeman in a dangling lobster pot?'

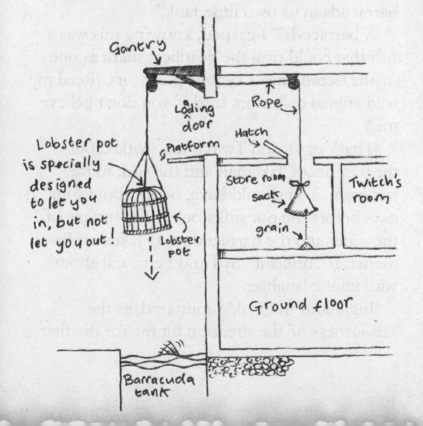

Gantry

Loading door

Rope

Hatch

Platform

Lobster pot is specially designed to let you in, but not let you out!

Store room

sack

Twitch's room

grain

Lobster pot

Ground floor

Barracuda tank

'It's simple,' guffawed Perce at his side. 'So simple even you should get it. We give him some grub and there he will stay quite unharmed until you return from Twitch's quest. But just to make sure you do return, we're gonna cut a tiny hole in that sack on the other end of the rope. It's full of grain and acts as a counter-weight to Jakeman in the pot. As the grain starts to trickle out of the little hole, the sack will get lighter and Jakeman's pot will drop closer to the water – where we keep a very hungry, man-eating barracuda in its own little tank!'

'A barracuda?' I gasped, knowing this was a fish that could rival the deadliest shark as one of the ocean's most vicious predators. (Read my wild animal collectors card if you don't believe me!)

'That's right, and Twitch has worked out the weights of Jakeman and the sack to the last gram. You should have, oooh, about four days before the pot sinks below the surface of the water and the barracuda gets Jakeman for dinner. It's brilliant!' Syd and Perce fell about with idiotic laughter.

'Ingenious but evil,' I muttered, as the seriousness of the situation hit me for the first

Barracuda

Barracudas are fearsome and voracious predators. They can grow up to 6 feet (1.8 metres) in length. They lie in wait in the shadows and ambush their prey. A barracuda can swim up to nearly 30 miles an hour. They have strong tearing jaws and their large mouths are full of huge, fang-shaped teeth with which they make long, jagged tears in their victim's skin. Barracudas are formidable hunters and, if they are hungry, these ferocious fish may attack and eat you!

WILD ANIMAL COLLECTORS CARDS

time. If I didn't go on this expedition for Twitch and bring back the prizes *pronto*, Jakeman would become supper for a ravenous barracuda; not only would I lose the best pal ever but he would never be able to show me how to get home to my mum and dad. 'You fiends!' I croaked.

'Seen enough?' asked Syd, sniggering. I nodded and the two men took me back down to Tristram Twitch.

Twitch was lying on his chaise longue. 'Now, what do you say, Charlie?' he asked with a sly grin. 'Fancy going on this little adventure?'

'How dare you do this to dear old Jakeman?' I said through gritted teeth. 'You give me no choice – I'll have to go adventuring for you and your silly girlfriend.'

'Oh, marvellous – I thought you might say that!' said Twitch, clapping his hands.

'But surely four days won't be enough to complete all three tasks?' I said, desperately.

'Four days is all you've got,' snapped Twitch, letting his toadying manner slip for a second. 'Aveline won't wait for ever. Now, if everything's settled, all that's left to do is introduce you to your travelling companion.'

'What travelling companion?' I cried, but Twitch didn't answer.

My Travelling Companion And The Hover-Sub

With dread, I followed the foppish fellow and his thuggish minions down some rickety stairs to another long room. At one end, a deep canal entered the warehouse by a brick arch in the wall. Rocking on the canal's choppy water sat the most incredible craft I have ever seen. It looked like some sort of prehistoric crab, and I knew straight away that it was one of Jakeman's miraculous machines.

The stubby-shaped craft was about six metres long. It had a domed glass cabin at the front and tapered back in a series of curved copper panels to a fanned metal tail at the rear. A soft light glowed behind the glass front and I could see a pair of high-backed leather seats and a flashing instrument panel. From either side of the windscreen there extended two metal arms which ended in vicious-looking claws. Oh boy – it was mega-cool!

'It's the Jakeman Chemical-powered Crustacean Hover-sub,' said a voice from behind us, and spinning around in surprise, I saw a girl dressed in overalls, wiping a gleaming bit of brass machinery with an oily rag. She was perhaps a year or two older than me, with a snub nose, a face sprinkled with freckles and her hair pulled into two untidy buns behind her ears. 'I've just got to put this widget back and we should be ready to go,' she added.

'Charlie, meet Philhomena, Jakeman's granddaughter and chief assistant,' said Twitch silkily. Jakeman's granddaughter!

'Philly,' corrected the girl. 'No one's called Philhomena nowadays.

You took your time, Charlie Small,' she said, giving me a cold look. 'If you're ready, we can push off.'

'Hi Philly, pleased to meet you,' I said, but she pretended not to hear me and crouched down to place the brass contraption in the open nose of the craft. I got the distinct impression that she was blaming me for something.

'My dear, there's no need to be unfriendly,' said Twitch. Then, turning to me he added, 'I have supplied maps and notes and diagrams to show you where to go and what to look out for. Philhomena knows how to pilot the craft, so you won't have to worry about that.'

'I should do,' mumbled Philly. 'I helped build the thing.'

'Well, if everybody's ready, I think it's time you got going!' said Twitch.

Philly

We Push Off ⟶

With my rucksack returned, I followed Philly
along a plank that led from the cobbled bank
of the waterway to an open hatch in the side of
the craft. She turned a great wheel that released
the air-locked door to the interior of the sub
and pushed it open. A tangle of pipes, gauges
and pistons gleamed in the gloomy interior.
Without a word, Philly led me past the mass of
machinery and opened another door and we
stepped into the glass-fronted cockpit.

We sat in a pair of seats behind a bank of
dials; Philly flicked a couple of switches and
pressed a button on the console. With a splutter
and cough the engines clattered into life. Then
the silent and sulky girl pushed the joystick
in front of her. An excited-looking Twitch
watched us as the hover-sub moved slowly
forward along the narrow waterway. As we
disappeared under the low, brick arch, he called
out above the noise: 'Hurry back with
my lovely loot. Toodle-
pip!' and fluttered his
lacy handkerchief in
a wave.

Toodle-pip!

Philly steered the hover-sub between the surrounding buildings. Steep walls towered above us on both sides, casting the channel into deep shadow. Then all of a sudden, we emerged into the brilliant sunshine of the busy harbour. Sailing ships and skiffs thronged the docks and the coarse, happy voices of the sailors reached us through the curved glass windscreen of our cockpit, like the hum from a swarm of busy bees.

The cabin was quite small, and instruments flashed like little heartbeats from every available surface. The long dashboard in front of us bristled with switches and levers, our course being plotted by tiny lights that beeped across three dark screens.

'If we're going to be stuck in this hover-sub for the next four days, we might as well try and be friends,' I said to Philly, but she totally ignored me and pretended to be busy with the controls.

'Is there anything I can do to help?' I asked.

'Shouldn't think so,' she muttered.

I sighed and started to play with some buttons on the arm of my chair. I pressed one and the chair whirred and clicked as it slowly tilted backwards. I pressed another button and it immediately started to get warm – a centrally heated chair-bed. Cool!

'This is mega!' I chuckled as I pushed the last button and the chair began to rock gently back and forth. Philly just tutted and gave me a look of disdain. As the  hover-sub slowly crossed the busy harbour, I got up and had a look around the rest of the cabin.

Directly behind us was a galley area with worktop and sink. A microwave oven and a hot drinks dispenser were built into the brushed steel walls and the whole back wall was made up of a series of cupboards and drawers that pulled out, revealing cans of baked beans and packets of microwavable meals; burgers and chips, fish fingers and pizzas. It was like an Aladdin's cave of the best grub ever!

I opened the door to the engine room.

'Don't touch anything,' grumbled Philly, as I

marvelled at the labyrinth of pipes and tubes. Great brass pistons hissed and pumped, turning a massive drive shaft that exited at the tail end of the sub. On the far side of the engine room was a narrow door and opening it, I discovered a chemical loo. Jakeman had really thought of everything!

'Look, this is daft. We really ought to try and get on together,' I said to Philly when I went back to the cockpit.

'There are some charts in that middle locker,' she said coldly, pointing to the steel wall behind us. 'And a list of the stupid presents we've got to get for that puffed-up twit, Twitch. Look them out and we can get started on this madcap mission.'

I went and got the pile of papers from the locker and, returning to my seat, unfolded the top sheet across my knees. It was a large map of a wide and stormy ocean, dotted with islands and rocks and sandbanks. Dividing the sea was a jagged line labelled *The Great Divide*. Beyond was the *Land of Legends*. See over the page for the actual map Twitch supplied us with.

'It looks pretty wild and dangerous,' I gulped.

'Oh, typical!' snapped Philly. 'We're not even

out of the harbour and you've started whinging! I thought you were supposed to be clever. I thought you were supposed to be a brilliant adventurer, a top-notch navigator and all round super-hero!'

'I never said . . .' I began, but Philly interrupted me again and I knew I wasn't going to be able to avoid an argument.

'Grandpa's always on about you,' said Philly. 'Charlie this; Charlie that. Gets on my flippin' nerves. And now, because of you, I've got to trek halfway across the world looking for a silly giant pearl or something!'

'Don't have a go at me,' I cried. 'It's not my fault.'

'Oh, and whose fault is it then?' yelled Philly. 'If it wasn't for you, Twitch and his twits wouldn't have Grandpa dangling over a tank as barracuda bait. He could well end up as fish food. If anything happens to him I'll never forgive you – you . . . you . . . boy! And all because Twitch wanted the great Charlie Small to help him.'

'That's not fair!' I yelled back. 'Setting off across an unknown ocean to try and retrieve three priceless objects is not my idea of fun, you

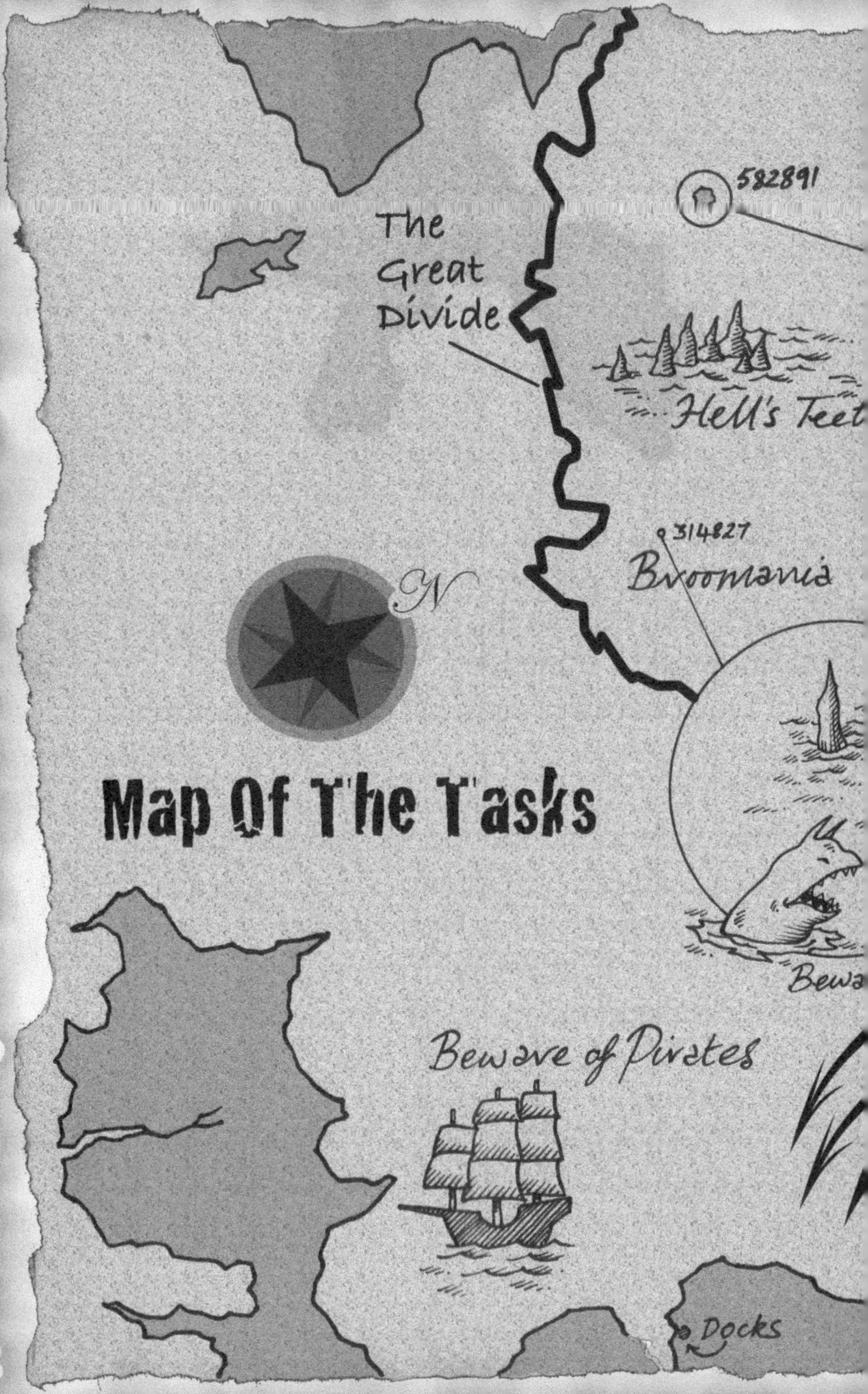

582891

The
Great
Divide

Hell's Teet

314827

Broomania

N

Map Of The Tasks

Bewa

Beware of Pirates

Docks

The Tiara

98994

Mayazapan

The Island of
Puwh. The tomb
may be protected by
an ancient curse

Menagerie

Tides

oyster beds
at 50,000 fathoms

onsters

The Land of
Legends

The
Great
Divide

know.' (Well, it is actually, but I thought it best not to mention it just then!) 'And when it comes to laying blame – if it wasn't for your grandpa, I wouldn't even be here at all.'

Philly went quiet, pressing her lips together and snorting through her nose. 'Yeah, whatever . . .' she began, and then went into a sulk.

We left the calm waters of the harbour and the engines of the hover-sub hummed faintly as we ploughed into the choppy waves of the open sea, sitting in a cross silence.

The Great Divide ← Oo, er!

For hours we sailed across the rough grey sea, heading north towards the area where the thick line of the Great Divide separated the map in two. All the places Twitch had mentioned seemed to be on the other side of this border. What on earth is the Great Divide, I wondered?

Eventually, Philly's frosty mood thawed a little and she started to talk.

'What did you make of Tristram Twitch?' she asked.

'At first I thought he was the biggest, most

feeble twit I've ever met,' I replied. 'But now I'm not so sure. How about you?'

Twitch is a big fathead!

'I wouldn't trust him as far as I could throw him,' said Philly. 'Sometimes he seems so comical and then he comes up with something like the barracuda tank, and you realize that beneath his silly exterior he's a very nasty man indeed.' Looking at me, she added seriously, 'We've got to succeed, Charlie, 'cos I have no doubt he'll really feed Grandpa to that fang-toothed fish.' I believed it too. 'Don't worry, Philly. We'll get Twitch's treasures for him and get home in time to save Jakeman. I promise.' But deep down inside, I wasn't so sure.

Just then Philly cried 'Look!' And up ahead I could see a massive, moving cloud lying on the sea, misting the horizon and climbing high into the slate blue sky. 'That's the Great Divide. Oh wow! Have you ever seen anything like it?'

There was a massive cloud lying on the sea!

I stared in awe at the boiling, shifting cloud bank. 'What exactly is this Great Divide?' I gasped.

'It's where two vast oceans meet. Their waters fight and swirl together in huge whirlpools and terrific thunderstorms,' explained Philly. 'It's the most treacherous stretch of water in the world and only one lone explorer has been known to have crossed it and survived. It's from him that all the stories of pearls and tiaras came from.'

'Oh!' I whispered in a small voice, wishing I hadn't asked. Now I was beginning to understand why Twitch didn't want to go on this adventure himself!

As we got closer we could see the waters getting rougher; jagged waves smashed against each other, making the surface of the ocean bubble and foam as if it were boiling. Seagulls were thrown about in the air as if they were scraps of newspaper blown on the wind, and our craft started to rock and pitch violently.

'Time to go into hover mode, I think,' said Philly. She pulled a lever, flicked a switch and immediately the hum from our engines increased and we lifted about a metre from the ocean's surface.

Now, out of the water, our craft was more stable. But then the winds started to increase, blowing us backwards and spinning us round, and the hovercraft thrusters began to scream and whine in protest.

'It's no good, we're going to have to get back in the water,' cried Philly above the noise of the wind. I marvelled at her piloting skills as she lowered the hover-sub carefully back onto the sea and once more we rode the high, churning waves.

Soon we were passing into the big, misty cloud and everything turned milky white. Rain poured from the air above and around us, churning the sea even more. Flashes of electricity pulsed at the heart of the giant cloud. It was impossible to see where we were going, and Philly had to watch the radar screen like a hawk, to check on our course.

All of a sudden, the mists parted and there in front of us was the Great Divide itself: a sinister stretch of dark water, spinning in a huge spiral, round and round and down and down like a giant, liquid helter-skelter.

'Look out. It's a whirlpool!' I cried, but we were too late. The waters grabbed our hover-sub in its

lightning flashed all around us →

We were swept into the whirlpool

strong spinning current and we were swept away. 'Yikes!' I cried, starting to panic as we tumbled over and over. We were going to be sucked right down to the bottom of the sea and smashed to pieces on the ocean floor.

Philly, though, remained calm. She threw switches; she turned dials; she throttled levers and fought with the joystick.

'Hold on to your seat!' she cried as we were drawn further into the whirlpool. Everything went dark as we were dragged below the surface like a spider being emptied with the bath water. Philly threw the joystick to the left and the hover-sub fought against the sinewy currents that tried to suck us down deeper and deeper into the roaring black waters.

Then the joystick was ripped from her hand and the hovercraft rolled and tumbled through the sea, over and over, with us dangling from our seatbelts like two rag dolls. The lights went out in the cabin, the roar of the engines ceased and we gradually stopped flipping, and floated in the inky blackness of the sea. Suddenly, my ears started to roar and pop as the hover-sub began to rise towards the surface like a cork. *POP!* We flew out into the air, and the hovercraft landed the right way up on the surface of the water.

'Are you OK?' I asked Philly nervously as the sea boiled around us. There was no reply. Oh no! If Philly was injured, we'd be in serious trouble. I had no idea how to drive this contraption of Jakeman's!

Then, 'Yeah! I'm OK, I think,' she said. 'I just bumped my head and went a bit woozy for a minute.' She fiddled with the switches on the dashboard and the lights in the cabin flickered back on and the engines spluttered into life. Then, '*Wow!*' we both exclaimed, looking out through the windscreen. 'We've done it!'

Beyond The Great Divide

The Land of Legends is an amazing place. It isn't sunnier exactly – the sky is actually quite overcast, but the colours look brighter and stronger. The sea is still grey, but it shines with an intense oily, blue sheen; the seagulls skimming the ocean's surface are so white they hurt your eyes; the seaweed floating on the waves is a bright, bilious green; it's as if the colour contrast has been turned right up on your telly – and you can see for miles and miles and miles.

'Weird!' I said. 'Everything looks the same but sort of different – if you know what I mean. I wonder if there are mythical monsters in this Land of Legends?'

'I've no idea. I hope not,' said Philly, rubbing her bruised head. 'I just want to get our tasks done and get back home. I'm not sure I'm cut out for a life of adventures.'

'But you were brilliant!' I cried, turning to Philly. 'The way you handled this machine over the Great Divide was a miracle!'

'Do you think so?' asked Philly with a shy smile.

'I should say so.'

'Thanks,' said Philly, blushing slightly. 'I'm sorry I was in such a foul mood earlier. I'm just worried about Grandpa.'

'I know,' I said. 'But he'll be all right, I'm sure. Come on, let's get these tasks done

'Do you think so?' asked Philly with a shy smile

and then we can go home. They can't be all that hard, can they?'

Oh boy, why won't I ever learn to keep my big mouth shut!

Philly revved up the engines and thrust the joystick forward, sending us ploughing through the sea then, changing once more to hover mode, we rose up and scooted along a metre above the waves.

ZOOOOM!

On Our Way To Broomania

Philly and I are on much friendlier terms after the dangers we faced crossing the Great Divide; her scowl has been replaced with a smile. What a relief!

I have just shuffled through the papers and found the original letter from Aveline to Twitch. What a nincompoop he is!

Three Tiddly Tasks For
My True-love, Tristram

Yuk! How revolting! ←

My dearest, darling twiddle-toes Tristram,

I know how much you adore me, and I can't say I blame you (Daddy has told me how utterly adorable I am since the day I was born, and he's _always_ right). You said you would go to the ends of the earth for me; face any dangers for me. Now's your chance to prove it, you brave heroic boy.

When I was little, Daddy always told me stories of the explorer who had travelled to the mythical Land of Legends and of all the wonderful treasures he'd seen beyond the Great Divide. Now _I_ want some of those treasures. Before I marry you, you must bring me three little tokens of your love. That's not too much to ask, is it?

Here is my wish list:

1) A gorgeous great globe of a pearl from the giant oyster beds only found in the legendary waters of Broomania. It doesn't have to be the _biggest_ pearl – one about the size of a tennis ball will do.

2) The famous diamond-encrusted tiara the explorer saw on the petrified Princess Penelope. According to his notes, her mummified body is somewhere in a temple on the ancient island of Purh. I would like to wear this trinket on our wedding day. I would look utterly, utterly magnificent.

3) A priceless, gold spine plucked from the back of the Golden Porcupine. There is only one of these wonderful creatures in existence, and he lives in the menagerie of the terrible and powerful Potentate of Mayazapan.

Good luck on your little trip, beloved, and hurry home with all my treats. Oh, by the way; if you haven't got them by the summer solstice, the wedding is off. I can't wait for you forever, you know.

Love from your utterly adorable Aveline
xxxxxxxxxxxxxxxxxxxxxxxxxxxxxxxxxxxxxxx
xxxxxxxxxxxxxxxxxxxxxxxxxxxxxxxxxxxxxxx
xxxxxxxxxxxxxxxxxxxxxxxxxxxxxxxxxxxxxxx
xxxxxxxxxxxxxxxxxxxxxxxxxxxxxxxxxxxxxxx
xxxxxxxxxxxxxxxxxxxxxxxxxxxxxxxxxxxxxxx
xxxxxxxxxxxxxxxxxxxxxxxxxxxxxxxxxxxxxxx
xxxxxxxxxxxxxxxxxxxxxxxxxxxxxxxxxxxxxxx
xxxxxxxxxxxxxxxxxxxxxxxxxxxxxxxxxxxxxxx

'Wow! Miss Spoiled Brat or what!' said Philly.

'What's the summer solstice?' I asked.

'It's the longest day of the year – four days away. That's the time limit Twitch was on about. So, we've got to get a move on, Charlie. First stop, Broomania, and task number one. What are the co-ordinates?'

I looked closely at Twitch's map and saw some numbers marked alongside the name. '314827,' I read.

'Could you tap them into that panel on the dashboard?' asked Philly. I carefully pressed the numbered buttons in front of me. With that, Philly flicked another switch and let go of the joystick. 'We're on autopilot now,' she said, stretching and yawning. 'It's a long way and we won't get there until tomorrow morning, even at top speed. I don't know about you, but I'm famished. Do you fancy something to eat?'

The sky is darkening outside, but we're sitting in the warm glow from the cabin lights. We have just heated a couple of burgers in the microwave and wolfed them down, followed by

Yum yum! Burgers for dinner

a mug of thick, hot, creamy chocolate from the drinks dispenser.

Philly can't stop yawning, and has flopped down in her chair and pulled a warm blanket up under her chin. She looks exhausted after her struggle to control the hover-sub through the Great Divide.

'Are there any dangers we can expect at Broomania?' I ask, but there is no reply. Philly is already fast asleep.

I Check My Explorer's Kit

The sun has slid below the horizon, turning the vast ocean orangey-yellow and making it appear to dance with flames. I have emptied my rucksack onto the floor. It is the first opportunity I've had to inspect my new explorer's kit (also a fully working jetpack!) since Mamuk gave it to me as a present.

My kit now contains:

1) My multi-tooled penknife
2) A ball of string
(about half a ball now!)
3) A water bottle (full)

← my metal water bottle

4) A telescope
5) A scarf (complete with bullet holes!)
6) An old railway ticket
7) This journal
8) A pack of wild animal collectors cards
(full of useful facts)
9) A glue pen
10) A glass eye (from the bravest friend
I have met on my travels so far: the
steam-powered rhinoceros)
11) The hunting knife, compass and torch
I found on the sun-bleached skeleton of
a lost explorer
12) The tooth of a monstrous mega-shark

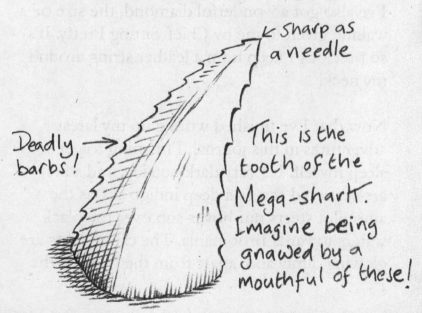

← Sharp as
a needle

Deadly →
barbs!

This is the
tooth of the
Mega-shark.
Imagine being
gnawed by a
mouthful of these!

13) A magnifying glass
14) A radio (crushed
by Bobo, but now
as good as new!)
15) My mobile phone
 with wind-up charger
16) The skull of a Barbarous Bat
17) A bundle of maps collected during
my travels
18) A bag of marbles
19) A plastic lemon full of lemon juice
20) A brand new lasso (to replace the one
I dropped down the fiery pit)

I've also got a wonderful diamond, the size of a
walnut, given to me by Chief Sitting Pretty. It's
so precious I keep it on a leather string around
my neck!

Now that I've finished writing up my latest
adventures in this journal, I'm going to get some
sleep myself. It's very dark outside, and stars
are scattered across a deep indigo sky as the
autopilot steers our hover-sub over the black
waters towards Broomania. The cabin lights are
glowing dimly and, apart from the hum of the

engines, it's very quiet.

Oh boy – I'm bushed! Since leaving my tent on the hills above the docks, I've been nabbed by Syd and Perce, enlisted by Tristram Twitch to do his dirty work and nearly sent crashing to the bottom of the ocean! Quite a busy day – I wonder what tomorrow will bring? I'll write more as soon as I can.

The Oyster Beds Of Broomania:

Oh yikes! If I thought *that* was a day full of danger, what happened when we dived down to the giant oyster beds was ten times worse . . .

I woke the next morning to the blinding light of a low sun streaming into the glass cockpit. Philly was already awake and checking the instruments on the dashboard.

'Not long now,' she said. 'Another hour and we'll be over the Broomanian oyster beds. You'd better grab some breakfast and check the papers for any more info on our destination.'

I helped myself to a glass of juice and a

banana from the fridge, and as we raced above the waves of the strange, oily-blue sea, I started

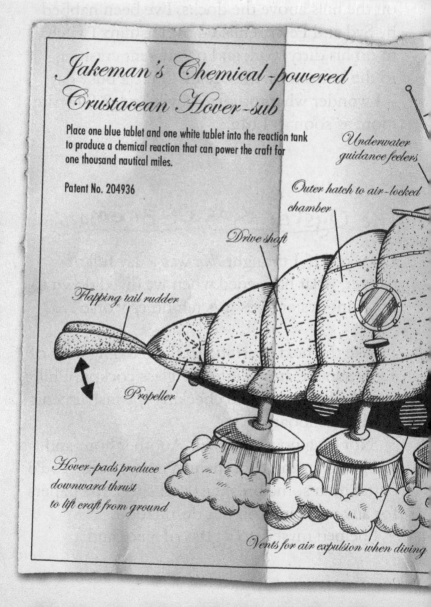

Jakeman's Chemical-powered Crustacean Hover-sub

Place one blue tablet and one white tablet into the reaction tank to produce a chemical reaction that can power the craft for one thousand nautical miles.

Patent No. 204936

Underwater guidance feelers

Outer hatch to air-locked chamber

Drive shaft

Flapping tail rudder

Propeller

Hover-pads produce downward thrust to lift craft from ground

Vents for air expulsion when diving

to look through the papers Twitch had left
for us. Amongst them I found a plan of the
Crustacean Hover-sub.

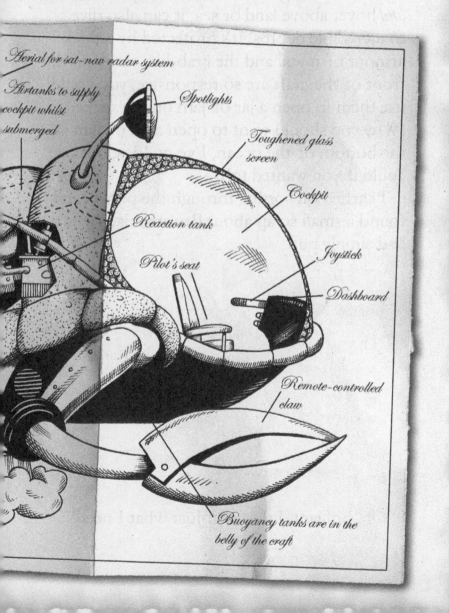

Aerial for sat-nav radar system

Airtanks to supply
cockpit whilst
submerged

Spotlights

Toughened glass
screen

Cockpit

Reaction tank

Joystick

Pilot's seat

Dashboard

Remote-controlled
claw

Buoyancy tanks are in the
belly of the craft

Studying the diagram I realized for the first time what an amazing vehicle it is. Not only can it plough through the water like a speedboat *and* hover above land or sea, it can also dive to incredible depths. It's protected by a thick armour of metal and the crab-like claws on the front of the craft are so responsive, you could use them to open a jar of jam on the seabed. (Why you should want to open a jar of jam at the bottom of the ocean, I've no idea, but you could if you wanted to!)

I carried on sorting through the papers and found a small scrap about Broomania. Twitch had simply put:

Known facts about Broomania

Nothing more than a spear of rock jutting out of the sea. Beware – Giant Oysters are very strong and have remarkably advanced brains for a mollusc. Approach with care.

Twitch

Oh, brilliant, I thought. Just what I need!

The rock looked like a beckoning finger

Soon a dark shape appeared on the horizon and the hover-sub turned and headed towards it. As we got nearer, I could see it was a tall shard of rock sticking out above the waves. It looked like a sinister, beckoning finger, and from Twitch's note I knew this *had* to be Broomania. All of a sudden, a hooter sounded from the dashboard; the hover-sub automatically came to a stop and, like a great fat bluebottle, landed gently on the surface of the choppy sea.

'We've arrived,' cried Philly. 'We should be directly above the giant oyster beds. It's time to go pearl diving, Charlie!'

'Is there a wetsuit on board?' I asked, somewhat nervously. I'd never been deep sea diving before and I knew Philly couldn't go, as she would have to stay on board to man the hover-sub.

'Oh no, you won't have to do any diving!' laughed Philly at my stricken face. 'I can retrieve the pearl from inside the sub, using the claws.' Phew!

Diving, Diving!

Philly turned a dial and there was a whooshing sound as air was driven from the sub's buoyancy tanks. Amidst a torrent of bubbles, we started to sink below the sea's surface. She pushed the joystick forward; the sub tilted and we dived down . . . and down . . . and down.

The water became dark and murky, so Philly turned the sub's two large spotlights on, illuminating an area about six metres ahead of us. Beyond our beams the ocean appeared jet-black, and it was a shock when strange fishes unexpectedly swam into view, gulping great mouthfuls of water, their multi-coloured bodies flashing in the shafts of light. Except for a low hiss from the air-tanks supplying the cockpit with oxygen, it was completely silent.

We continued to dive, deeper and deeper.

It was really eerie and I found myself holding my breath, waiting for some terrible phantom to appear from the black water.

All of a sudden, Philly cried out, shattering the silence and making my heart race. 'There they are!'

Directly below us was a field of massive oyster shells, standing up from the seabed as tall as garden sheds. They glowed a pale, rusty white in the beam from our headlights and looked ghastly and ghostly; like a cemetery of ancient, weathered gravestones. There were hundreds of them, all swaying gently in the swell of the current; some with their shells firmly shut, others standing slightly ajar. Shoals of silent fish weaved and bobbed amongst the oysters, stopping to nibble at the mossy beards that hung from the lips of the shells.

'Spooky!' I whispered to myself.

'Don't worry, this won't take long,' said Philly, who didn't seem at all bothered about being thousands of fathoms below the surface in the pitch black. She gave the joystick a jog and we edged forward until the hover-sub sat directly over a large, gnarly shell. Picking up a small hand-held console and plugging it into the dashboard, she started to twiddle two little sticks with her thumbs. Immediately the sub's great crab-like claws started to move. They extended down towards the oyster, and with surprising accuracy Philly steered one of the claws into the shell's narrow opening.

'Now all I've got to do is force it wider, grab the pearl with the other claw and it's on to task number two,' she said proudly. 'Easy peas . . .'

SNAP! CRUNCH!

Suddenly, there was the horrible screeching sound of metal being crushed, and our sub was yanked violently forward. The oyster had snapped its shell closed, trapping the sub's claw inside and crushing it between the hard, serrated edges of its shell. Wow, it was strong!

'Oh heck!' cried Philly. 'What now?'

'Try to free it with the other claw,' I said, trying not to panic.

Philly steered the other claw towards the oyster, but as she did so the creature gave a mighty jerk and we were yanked forward again. Then the oyster started to rock back and forth, throwing our useless sub around as easily as if it were waving a handkerchief. The metal skin of the hover-sub screamed and squealed in protest, as we were thrown this way and that inside the cabin.

'Help, Charlie!' cried Philly. 'Much more of this and our sub will be ripped apart!'

Then the oyster stopped rocking and the sub came to rest. It floated in the water, still held by one claw in the vicious mouth of the giant shell. Philly and I sat, panting for breath and shaken, staring at each other with wide, terrified eyes.

'There's nothing for it,' said Philly, looking at me apologetically. 'You're going to have to swim out and try and free us by hand. Quick, before it starts up again and we're shaken to pieces!'

'What?' I cried.

'You've got to be joking! How on earth am I going to be able to loosen the oyster's iron-like grip by hand?'

I Have To Go Deep Sea Diving (Yikes!)

Five minutes later, I was standing in the cockpit feeling a right twit in a wetsuit two sizes too big for me.

'Very smart!' sniggered Philly.

'Don't start,' I muttered.

'Look, you'll be fine. Take a spanner and if all else fails, you'll have to unbolt the claw and we'll leave it behind.'

'OK,' I said, slipping the spanner into the utility belt around my waist. 'Now, where are my oxygen tanks?'

'Oh, we don't have any of them,' said Philly. 'But we've got one of these. Grandpa made it.' And she handed me what looked like a snorkel.

'Snorkels are no good when you're at the bottom of the sea,' I cried.

'You're right. It wouldn't be any good if it were a *normal* snorkel, but it's not – look,' and Philly pointed to the end of the device. It had a series of slits cut into it, and inside was a spiral of tubes and some padded discs. 'As you breathe, water is sucked through the slits and passes down the special tube which extracts the oxygen from the water and then filters it. It's brilliant – it kind of works like a fish's gills and you should be able to stay under water indefinitely!'

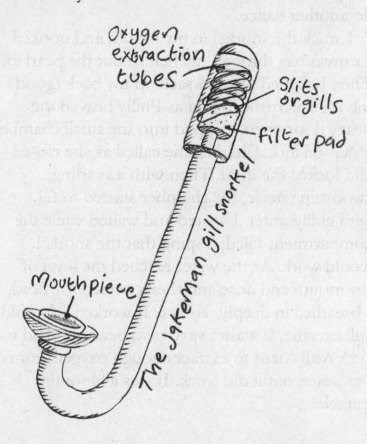

Oxygen
extraction
tubes

Slits
or gills

filter pad

Mouthpiece

The Jakeman gill snorkel

'Wow, that's brilliant! You have tested it though, haven't you?'

'Oh, of course. Grandpa tried it in the bath for a couple of minutes and he said it was fine!'

'A couple of minutes in the bath – is that all?'

'Oh Charlie, you are a worrier,' said Philly, turning the big wheel to the air-lock door. 'Come on, you'd better go before the oyster decides to do another dance.'

I stuck the snorkel in my mouth and hooked a canvas bag through my belt to put the pearl in. Then I slipped my rucksack on my back (good job it's waterproof!) and as Philly heaved the heavy door open, stepped into the small chamber.

'Good luck, Charlie,' she called as she closed and locked the door. Then with a swirling, swooshing noise, the chamber started to fill with chilly water. I waited and waited while the compartment filled, hoping that the snorkel would work. As the water reached the level of my mouth and nose and then covered my head, I breathed in deeply. *Yee-hah!* It worked – I could still breathe. It wasn't very easy, because I had to suck really hard to extract enough oxygen from the water, but it did work. It was a bloomin' miracle!

After what seemed like ages, the outer hatch opened and I pushed off from the floor and swam out into the ocean depths, leaving a trail of silver bubbles from the snorkel in my wake. Just in front of me was the giant oyster, caught in the beams from the sub's powerful spotlights. I quietly swam up alongside the shell.

Nabbed!

First I decided to see if I could open the shell, very gently, by hand.

I curled my fingers into the narrow gap and tried to ease the two massive halves apart. Nothing happened – the oyster seemed as solid as a lump of concrete. So, carefully getting the heel of my flipper behind one edge, I pulled the other side as hard as I could with *both* hands. Again nothing happened. Darn it – the oyster was super-strong! Then, getting rather impatient and careless, I took the hunting knife from my explorer's kit, jammed it into the gap and tried to lever the shell open.

Whoa! With a quick twist the oyster prised the knife from my grasp; a second later the knife

flew out again in two useless halves. Churning
up a swirling storm of sand, the oyster sent jets
of bubbling water shooting out from inside
its shell. I was in danger of sending the oyster
into another rage. Then I noticed that the noise
of the roaring bubbles from the angry oyster
sounded just like the growl of a grumpy dog.
I began to stroke the side of the oyster's shell
as if I were petting a pooch. Unbelievably the
oyster immediately stopped spitting out water.
I stroked the shell a bit more and gave it some
gentle pats, and the creature relaxed completely,
opening its shell and letting our sub's damaged
claw float from its grip! I was just about to
turn and give the thumbs up to Philly, when
something flashed from deep inside the oyster. I
gasped. It was a pearl – a pearl as big as a melon!

Without thinking, I plunged my hand inside.
Stretching as far as I could, I managed to get
my fingers around the smooth white globe and
lifted it gently from its fleshy bed. *Got it!* I cried
to myself. But I celebrated too soon, because as
I lifted my arm out, the shell gently closed again,
trapping my wrist between its hard serrated
edges. No! I pulled and heaved and punched
and prodded, but the shell wouldn't budge. Oh,

brilliant, I had freed the sub, but now *I* was
stuck!

I tried stroking the oyster shell again, but the
creature wasn't stupid; it had got what it wanted
– me! The two halves of the shell started to
move against each other and I felt myself being
dragged inside the mean mollusc! *Oh help!* I
twisted round to signal to Philly. Now she would
have to try and rescue me!

Philly was standing pressed up against the
glass of the cockpit, a look of absolute horror
on her face. But she wasn't looking at me – she
was pointing frantically over my shoulder. What
was it? I looked round and, oh no, I was in real
trouble now!

Electric Eel Attack! ⚡

Shooting out of the gloom came a huge, horned eel — a streak of malevolent muscle that fizzed like an electric cable! It was striped like a tiger and as long and thick as a tree trunk. Yikes, it was a real monster!

The eel's mouth was open in a wide, terrifying grin, exposing its nasty-looking, needle-sharp teeth. Protruding from the eel's brow were two pointed horns that crackled and sparked with electricity, lighting up the creature's evil-eyed stare.

My heart started to beat hard, like a roll on a snare drum. If those fizzing horns touched me, I would fry like a rasher of bacon! I took a gulp of air through my snorkel but it was so hard to suck enough oxygen in, I began to feel dizzy. I tried to yank my arm free, but by now I was stuck fast up to the elbow. Then, tucking its head down like a bull, the eel charged. Bloomin' heck! I thought, *I'm done for!*

As the eel thundered towards me, I managed to roll out of the way at the last minute, and the monster hit the oyster a glancing blow. We

span around in a crazy torrent of bubbles, but the mollusc didn't let go. The eel fizzed with anger and attacked again, this time giving me no chance to avoid its gaping mouth. As it snapped its jaws closed I kicked with all my strength, hoping to fend the beast off. It didn't work – but luckily all it got was a mouthful of my flipper!

The eel pulled with all its might, stretching the flipper further and further. The oyster pulled the other way and I thought I was going to be ripped in half. Then two things happened. My stretched flipper snapped off and whacked the eel a mighty blow around its chops, and Philly powered the hover-sub past the oyster, giving it a sound *thwak* with its good claw!

The oyster shell cracked like an egg, from one side to the other, and released me from its grasp. As the oyster reeled from the claw's hefty blow, its precious and massive pearl was thrown out and sank to the seabed. I dived down and retrieved it. Popping the prize

The pearl shot out of the oyster.

It was as big as a melon!

into the canvas bag hanging from my belt, I swam desperately for the sub's hatch.

But the eel was after me again, racing from the murky depths and sending out huge neon bolts of jagged electricity. *Oh help!* Then I had an idea: I didn't know if they worked underwater, but it was worth a try. I clicked the button-pad on my rucksack straps; the mini-jet thrusters on the bottom of my backpack roared into life, and with a massive explosion of bubbles I shot towards the sub like a torpedo. *Yee-hah!*

I was fast, but the eel was just as quick, and I was still fumbling with the handle to the sub's hatch when it was on me once again. It zoomed up close, opened its vast mouth and I shut my eyes, waiting to be gobbled up – but nothing happened. I opened my eyes again and saw the eel looking surprised, pain flashing across its face as it was yanked backwards. It tried to attack again, but it couldn't quite reach me. I looked down towards the seabed and saw that the damaged oyster had grabbed the tip of the eel's long, slimy tail. With a look of pure evil in its tiny eyes, the eel dived down to deal with the snapping shellfish. Phew, would you believe it – I'd been saved by the giant oyster that was trying to eat me!

As the eel attacked the oyster in a frenzy of bubbles below, I threw up the sub's hatch, dived inside and brought it slamming down behind me. Just in time; the eel managed to get free and rushed at the sub, striking like a snake. Its teeth clamped around the porthole in the hatch door and it tried to gnaw its way through the metal skin of our hover-sub. But the sub's armoured skin was too strong.

With a loud whooshing noise, the water began to drain from the compartment. Then the air-lock door swung open and Philly was helping me into the engine room.

'That was brilliant, Charlie!' she cried. 'I would have been petrified but you looked as cool as a cucumber!'

'Uh! Was . . . nothing,' I panted. I couldn't say any more – I was so scared I had lost the power of speech!

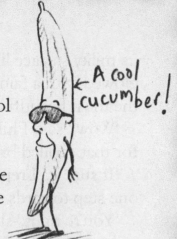

← A cool cucumber!

The Pearl Of The Ocean

Philly ran back to the pilot's seat, fired up the engines and we zoomed off through the water. The eel was still stubbornly clamped to the side of the sub, but with a few power thrusts we managed to shake it off and then shot up through the grey-green sea until we were floating on top of the sparkling ocean again.

When I'd got my breath and my voice back, we studied our prize. Turning the bag upside down, I rolled the enormous pearl onto a cushion and both Philly and I gaped at its splendour. The precious stone was a soft, silvery white, with the palest hints of purples and greens that seemed to move and shift over its milky surface like oil in a puddle. The orb glowed with a faint luminescence; it was one of the most beautiful things I'd ever seen.

'Wow!' said Philly. 'What a corker – pity it's for that spoiled brat, Aveline.'

'It sure is,' I replied. 'But just think of it as one step towards saving your grandpa.'

'You're right,' she said. 'Let's get to the next task; getting the tiara from the mummified princess. I think we'd better refuel before we go any further. Could you do that while I set the co-ordinates for Purh? There should be a row of instructions near the tank.'

I went through to the engine room as Philly powered up the hover-sub. Next to the reaction tank was an information panel, and after reading this I slid out a small drawer set into the wall. Inside were two lines of tablets, one row blue and the other white. Taking one pill of each colour, I yanked a release handle and lifted a panel on top of the tank. It opened with a loud hiss, and a small puff of coloured steam escaped that smelled strongly of pear drops. *Phwoar!* Checking the instructions again, I dropped the tablets inside and closed and locked the lid. According to Jakeman's diagram of the hover-sub, that should be enough fuel for one thousand nautical miles. Incredible! Much handier than having to find a petrol station in the middle of the wild ocean!

I went back to the cabin and flopped down in my seat next to Philly. I was absolutely exhausted after my run-in with the giant oyster and the electric eel.

Pills are put in slots and they slide down into the tank

Hatch

FUEL TANK

'All done,' I said and Philly pushed the joystick forward. We accelerated to cruising speed and she tapped in the next set of co-ordinates and switched the hover-sub over to autopilot.

'Next stop, the island of Purh and the Mummy's Tomb!'

Phoning Home

It was a long, long way to the Island of Purh. We zoomed along all afternoon and into another night. After a tea of beans on toast, Philly dozed fitfully in her seat and I took the mobile from my explorer's kit and phoned home.

I had hoped the next time I spoke to Mum I would be standing in our kitchen eating one of her delicious homemade rock cakes, but it seems I will have to wait a little bit longer before that happens.

'Charlie? Is that you?' said Mum. 'Is everything all right?' I knew exactly what she was going to say; it was the same every time I'd phoned her since my adventures began. She seems to be in a different time zone to me and, even though I'd been gone for four hundred years, not a single day had passed for Mum – and she was still expecting me home in time for my tea!

Mmm! rock cakes

'Everything's fine, Mum,' I said. 'I'm just going across the ocean in a crustacean hover-sub to steal some priceless wedding presents from a mummified corpse and a power-mad potentate!'

'Ooh! Sounds wonderful, dear,' she replied. 'Oh, here's your dad just come in. Now remember, don't be late for tea and pick up a pint of milk from the shops on your way back. Bye.'

'Mum, I said I was in a . . .' but Mum had already hung up. Never mind; at least I know she's not worrying about me. It would be nice to get back home and have a proper conversation, though; tell her about my adventures and show her all the things I've collected.

Philhomena

As our long journey carried on into the morning, I wrote up our latest adventures in my journal. Then, whilst eating breakfast, I listened as Philly told me all about herself, and how she came to be her grandpa's assistant.

Philhomena is ten years old and her dad,

Aloysius, was an inventor just like Jakeman. When Philly was five years old, Jakeman and her dad invented a huge hot air balloon that was capable of going into space – or so they thought!

Philly could remember the day of the balloon's maiden flight; she could remember her dad and mum stepping into the glass-domed capsule that hung below the bulging, billowing balloon. Philly's mum insisted on going as well, as she liked to share in all her husband's adventures, but it was thought too risky to take a five-year-old into space, so Philly stayed behind.

To the sound of the town's brass band, Philly and Jakeman and a crowd of well-wishers waved the intrepid couple off. The guy-ropes were released and the monster balloon floated gently up into the clear blue sky, higher and higher and higher – and that was the last Philly saw of her mum and dad.

The test flight was only supposed to last a week, but the week turned into months and the months into years and Jakeman finally had to admit that something had gone wrong. He still believes the two balloonists will come back though, and always tells Philly to *never* give up hope.

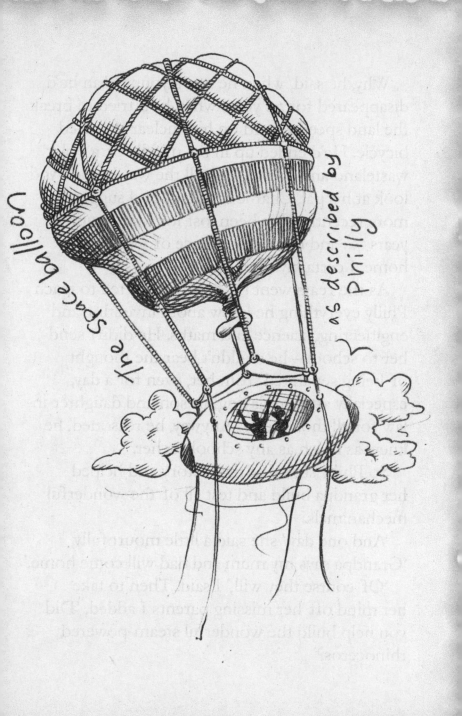

as described by Philly

the space balloon

Why, he said, when he was a young man he'd disappeared for *ten* years when he'd tried to break the land speed record on his nuclear-powered bicycle. He'd ended up in the middle of a polar wasteland and had to walk all the way home! And look at his pal, Charlie Small, he had suggested more recently. He's been lost for four hundred years . . . and has every chance of getting back home. I certainly hope so!

As the years went by, Jakeman started to teach Philly everything he knew about inventing and engineering, science and maths. He didn't send her to school – he couldn't bear the thought of being separated from her, even for a day, especially after mislaying his son and daughter-in-law for all those years. Anyway, he reasoned, he knew as much as any schoolteacher.

So Philly stayed at the factory and helped her grandpa build and test all of the wonderful mechanimals.

'And one day,' she said a little mournfully, 'Grandpa says my mum and dad will come home.'

'Of course they will,' I said. Then to take her mind off her missing parents I added, 'Did you help build the wonderful steam-powered rhinoceros?'

'Oh yes,' said Philly, cheering up instantly. 'That was really tricky to get right. Our first few rhinos exploded and blew a hole right through the factory roof.'

'The steam-powered rhino was one of the best mechanimals ever,' I said. 'I found it near Gorilla City and rode it across the great grass plain. A giant constricting snake attacked us and the rhino battered it into snake burgers – but was crushed to pieces itself in the ferocious struggle. Look, I kept a souvenir.' I took the rhino's glass eye from my rucksack and showed it to Philly. 'That's just about all that was left of it.'

'Poor thing,' said Philly, turning the green glass sphere between her fingers. 'At least it helped you though. It was built to be strong and brave.'

The rhino's eye

All of a sudden, the warning hooter sounded on the dashboard.

'We're here,' cried Philly, as the hover-sub slowly descended to rest on the sea. We'd been so busy talking that neither of us had noticed we'd been approaching a tall, craggy black island, and now it's sitting about a mile in front of us, looking like a pile of melted candle wax.

I must stop writing because we'll be landing on Purh any minute, and who knows what dangers will be waiting to greet us there! *Oh yikes!* I'm starting to get butterflies in my tummy. I'll write more later on . . . if I can!

The Island Of Purh

Wow! What an adventure!

With the hover-sub in boat mode, we circled the towering black island, looking for a place to go ashore. As Philly steered the boat I checked Twitch's notes about Purh. Again the facts are pretty sketchy:

Purh

It is said the Princess of Purh has been dead for two thousand years and her mummified body has lain in the island's temple ever since. It is forbidden to enter the temple and there are rumours of strange curses visiting anyone who tries. No one knows if the island is guarded or not, so be very, very careful. So glad it's not me going on this trip!

Twitch

'Sounds fun, I don't think!' murmured Philly as we continued to skirt the coastline, but the rocks rose vertically from the sea and there was no natural harbour or beach.

'Look!' I cried, pointing to the top of a tall column of rock that rose from one end of the island like a crooked church spire. Around the top of the column were a series of holes, and in each opening I could see the silhouette of a figure peering out. 'The island *is* guarded!' I took the telescope from my rucksack, lifted it to my eye and gasped in shock.

Peering from each lookout hole was an

eyeless, grinning skeleton. Each had a bony
hand curled around the hilt of a deadly-looking
sword.

'Jeepers creepers!' I cried, passing the
telescope to Philly. 'It looks like the island is
defended by a band of living skeleton sentries.
There's no way we can tackle those. What are we
going to do?'

Philly focused the telescope and stared
through it for the longest time.

'Well?' I asked. 'How are we going to get past
them?'

'We'll *walk* straight past them, Charlie,' she
grinned. 'They're not alive – they've been dead
for centuries. Have another look – they don't
move an inch!'

I felt really foolish as I trained the telescope
on the lookout points. Philly was right; the
skeletons stood stock-still. They were nothing
more than a pile of old bones! 'Sorry,' I blushed.

'Never mind about that,' Philly said, pointing.
'Look over there!'

I followed the direction of her finger and
saw two frayed ropes snaking down the side of
the cliff. The ropes dropped all the way down
to where a rickety wooden gondola rested on a

The scary skeletons grinned from their lookout posts

jetty sticking out into the foaming sea.

'That's our way up!' she cried and steered the boat towards the landing stage.

We secured our boat to the jetty as sea birds screamed and cawed above our heads. The waves boomed as they crashed around nearby rocks, sending big plumes of spray high into the air. Clambering out of our sub and into the dilapidated gondola, we heaved on one of the frayed ropes and the cradle started to lift us up the side of the cliff.

'I think we'd better test the strength of the ropes first,' suggested Philly, and looking at the worn and tattered cables I readily agreed. When we were a few metres from the ground we gingerly jumped up and down inside the gondola. It swayed violently and the ropes groaned in protest, but they held fast and we decided to carry on.

Pulleys squeaked and the cradle shuddered as we gradually left the pounding sea far below. It was all going well until about halfway up the cliff we saw a large nest – suddenly a Blue-footed Booby bird swooped down, brushing Philly's hair with its wide wings. (See my sketch of the pesky dive-bombing bird!) The bird rushed at us again, squawking madly and this time catching Philly a sharp blow to her head. She stumbled backwards, teetering over the low side of the cradle.

The bothersome
Booby bird

'Charlie!' she
screamed, and I just
managed to grab her by the
arm before she tipped over the side.

'Phew! Thanks,' she gasped and we kept
pulling up as fast as we could. Our creaking
gondola climbed quickly up the cliff and we left
the Booby nest far behind us.

'That was close!' I cried, breathing a huge sigh
of relief.

Soon we arrived at a platform built out
from the cliff top, about ten metres below the
skeleton's lookout holes, and we stepped onto
Purh Island.

At The Gates Of The Temple

A series of steps near the platform led up to the high, spire-like column of the skeletal sentries, but Philly had been right. No unearthly gang came clattering down the steps after us. They were all long dead. Perhaps they'd only been put there to deter visitors to the island; people like us, who'd come to find the diamond-encrusted tiara of the legendary princess!

The wind howled across the flat terrain below us and shrieked between the crags on the high ground. The whole place seemed to be moaning and groaning like a tormented ghost. We were high up on a lip of tall, craggy rocks that encircled the island and sloped down in a series of jagged peaks to a flat central plateau. Not one tree or blade of grass could be seen; the land was entirely barren and completely empty – apart from one lonely pyramid that stood right in the centre.

'Look, that must be the Princess of Purh's temple,' I said. 'That's where we've got to go!'

'Yes, and what a dump it is!' exclaimed Philly. 'C'mon. Let's not hang about.'

We climbed down to the central plain and, shielding our eyes from the clouds of dust and sand being carried by the wind, stepped out on the long walk to the pyramid. It rose from the flat-bottomed basin like the discarded building block of a giant baby.

The sandstorm was terrible and after a while I tied my holey scarf around my face to keep the sand from my mouth and eyes, and Philly did the same with one of the grubby rags she kept in her dungarees. We tucked our heads down and carried on. We had no idea what to expect; the closer we got to the temple, the more my heart raced.

The entrance to the pyramid

Eventually we reached the sloping base of the pyramid and as we turned one of the corners everything went quiet; at last we were out of the constant, battering wind and sand. Here we found a large columned porch protruding from the side of the temple. A wide flight of steps led up to some massive wooden doors, which were guarded by a pair of carved stone lions. Strange ancient symbols were etched on the high stone lintel above the doors, but neither Philly nor I could make head or tail of them; they just looked like a lot of scribbles.

Hanging over one of the large ring handles, though, was a notice that we *could* read.

'Well?' Philly asked. 'What shall we do now?'

'We've got to go on,' I said, although I was starting to get nervous, for who knows what sort of hellhound might be guarding the pyramid of Purh! I turned the handle and pushed the great door. It didn't budge. I pushed

KEEP OUT
by order of
Pyramid Security Services PLC
Danger! Danger!
BEWARE OF THE DOG!

harder, but it was no good.

'The doors are locked,' I said. 'And there doesn't seem to be a keyhole. What are we going to do?'

'Maybe there's a secret switch or something, like in fairy tales. It is the Land of Legends after all!' said Philly, and she started to press the metal studs that decorated the doors. 'No, these are no good.'

'This must be it,' I cried, pushing and pulling at a stone in the doorframe that stood proud of all the others, but this didn't work either. 'Darn it! It's set solid. There's got to be a way in, or our mission is doomed.'

We looked over the doors again, but couldn't see anything that might work as a secret lock. We tried drumming *rat-tat-a-tat-tat, tat tat* with the big metal knocker; we tried shouting 'Open Sesame!' like people do in storybooks, but neither worked. Then Philly walked up to one of the stone lions. 'What about these? Maybe one of their eyes presses in or something.'

The lion statues stood on their back legs, front paws raised and their sharp, stone claws extended. Their mouths were open in wild roars, and clamped between the long grey fangs

was a granite ball. We
pressed the lions' noses,
pulled their ears and
tried to move their
tails up and
down like levers,
but nothing happened.

'This is useless,' I said in
frustration. 'We'll never
get inside!'

'I think I've got it!'
cried Philly. 'The ball in
this lion's mouth is loose.
Look!' And she rolled the
ball around behind its long, granite fangs.

One of the
stone lions

'Give it a shove,' I said, racing over. Philly
gave the stone sphere a mighty push and it
rolled noisily along the lion's tongue and, with a
rumble, the ball dropped out of sight down its
throat.

We held our breath, waiting to see if
something would happen. We could hear the
heavy ball slowly rolling along under the ground,
backwards and forwards as if it were travelling
along a zigzag drainpipe. Every so often there
was a grating sound as if a stone were being

moved, then a clunk as the ball seemed to drop down to another level and then rumble on its way again. There was a final grating click and then silence.

Philly and I stared at each other. Then, with an excruciating *CREEAAK*, the great wooden doors slowly opened to reveal a long empty corridor lit by strong shafts of sunlight that poured in through apertures high up in the pyramid's walls.

'Brilliant! You've done it!' I cried, nervously looking for signs of a vicious guard dog. 'Oh! It's as quiet as a tomb.'

'It *is* a tomb, silly,' said Philly.

'I mean there's no sign of a guard dog. Come on.'

But the second I stepped over the threshold, a bullet-headed ball of barking, baying fury came bolting from behind a pillar towards me, its claws scrabbling and slipping on the

94

smooth stone floor. The fearsome-looking mutt snapped its slavering jaws and I leaped onto the base of a nearby column, hanging on for dear life as the animal growled and gnashed at me, leaping up to try and sever my foot with its knife-like teeth.

Mad Dog! "00"

'*Yikes!*' I cried, trying desperately to shin out of reach up the column. 'Philly, take cover!' But Philly was rooted to the spot, staring at the deranged dog. Its hairless back gleamed like a polished leather armchair; its muzzle and fangs shone like silver and its tiny eyes flashed red like little LED lights. It was the scariest dog I'd ever seen!

'Philly!' I repeated, 'watch out!' For now Philly had gone completely bonkers and was creeping towards the animal as it bounced up and down below me. Then to my horror, she reached a hand out towards the dog . . . and with a little brass key, unlocked a narrow lid on the dog's back. She flipped the lid open and turned a small dial! The dog immediately sat down and started to wag its tail.

'It's OK, you can come down now,' said Philly, looking up at me with a grin. 'It's only Mad Dog!'

'What do you mean?' I panted, gasping for breath as I slid back to the ground.

'He's one of ours!' said Philly. 'A Jakeman Mechanical-Automatic-Deterrent Guard Dog, or MAD Dog for short. Solar-powered!'

I breathed a huge sigh of relief. Now I could *see* the dog was man-made. His snout shone like metal because he was metal; his hide was made of padded, stitched leather and his eyes were two glowing red lights!

'I wonder how he got here – and how come he attacked me and not you?' I asked.

metallic muzzle →

Stuffed leather body ↗

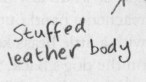

'The pyramid security firm must've bought him from our mail-order catalogue. He didn't attack me because all our guard dogs have a built-in image recognition system, and Grandpa has programmed them not to attack me or him.' As Philly explained, she knelt down, took a screwdriver from her dungarees and made some fine adjustments to a row of screw-heads under the flip-up panel. Then she pressed a button. With a click and a whirr, like a camera taking a picture, the dog's eyes flashed briefly.

'Right, that should do it,' she said. 'Mad Dog won't attack you any more.' She turned the

MAD DOG!

Solar panel

Metal feet and claws

control dial to its original setting, and Mad Dog leaped to his feet. I took a cautious step back, but he just wagged his tail and looked up at me with a lopsided grin as if to say, *what on earth are you so scared about?*

'Come on, Mad Dog,' said Philly. 'Do you know where the princess's mummy is?' Mad Dog yapped excitedly and waddled off down the corridor, his steel claws tapping against the floor. At the far end, a flight of stairs descended into darkness and we followed the mechanical pooch.

The Labyrinth Of Fear

The corridor stretched far into the distance, lit by eternal flaming torches screwed to the walls. Mad Dog pattered along at a trot and Philly and I had to jog to keep up. At the far end, the passage was crossed by another corridor. We followed the pooch for what seemed like hours, first to the left and then to the right – until we had lost all sense of direction. Each passage was so like the last that it wasn't long before both of us started to feel befuddled and confused.

'Don't lose sight of Mad Dog, or we'll be in real trouble,' said Philly shakily. 'We'll never find our way out of here.'

Just as she said this, she tripped over a lone skeleton stretched out on the floor and covered in swathes of ancient cobwebs. Its bony hand held an old map which I pulled from its grasp and tried to read. But most of the lines had completely faded away.

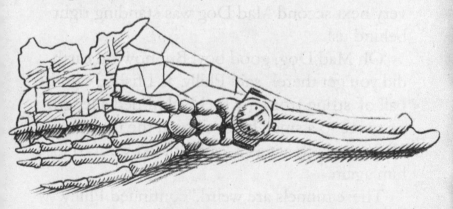

'I don't know how this man got so far, but he couldn't have made it through the maze, poor soul,' said Philly quietly. 'We're so lucky we've got Mad Dog to guide us . . . Oh Charlie! Where is Mad Dog?'

I looked up and down the passage but it was completely deserted. *Oh no!*

'Mad Dog!' we cried. 'Mad Dog, come here.' We listened but couldn't hear a thing.

'Oh Charlie, we'll be stuck down here forever!' said Philly.

'Don't panic,' I said, starting to get really scared. 'Don't . . .' Just then we heard a muffled bark in the far distance.

'Here, boy! Come here!' I cried. *Woof woof!* The sound came from miles away . . . but the very next second Mad Dog was standing right behind us!

'Oh Mad Dog, good boy! But how on earth did you get there?' said Philly, as I fished out the ball of string from my rucksack. I tied a length of twine to a small brass ring on the top of Mad Dog's neck, to act as a lead. I didn't want to lose him again.

'These tunnels are weird,' continued Philly. 'Distances seem all stretched out one minute and squashed up the next.'

The weird corridors were about to get a *whole* lot weirder! Now they really started to play tricks on us. As we hurried along the endless and identical passages, the flagstones on the floor seemed to get bigger and bigger and the walls grew taller – or was it that Philly and I were shrinking? It certainly felt as if we were getting smaller, and it wasn't a nice feeling at all!

It felt as if we were shrinking

'Oh my goodness!' cried Philly, reaching out for my hand. 'I don't like this, Charlie.'

I was starting to feel sick, as if we were going down very fast in a lift. Now the floor buckled and bulged beneath our feet, making us stumble and grab at the walls for support. 'Help! It's like a bad dream!' I groaned.

We turned into a corridor that looked a mile long, but two steps later we banged into the far wall. We followed Mad Dog into another hallway and here the walls and floor were twisted at crazy angles. Now it felt as if we were walking on the walls and then upside down on the ceiling. Philly and I held hands to steady ourselves, as we followed the mechanical pet through an arch that seemed to open up at our feet.

As we stepped through the arch, all of a sudden we were standing the right way up, the room stayed the same size and the floor stopped rising and falling like an ocean wave. Our wobbly legs gave way and both of us sank to the floor, trying to regain our sense of balance and scale. Ahead of us was a heavy, carved wooden door. Mad Dog yapped and sat down.

'Are you OK?' I asked and Philly nodded her head.

'This must be the princess's burial chamber,'

she said, getting unsteadily to her feet again and going over to the entrance. Like the main gates, this door had symbols carved on it. They looked like some sort of warning. I copied them down into this book – can you decipher them?

'At least there's a key in this door,' said Philly, taking hold of the massive wrought-iron key that stuck out of the lock. It turned with a dull clunk. 'Are you scared?'

You bet I was. My throat had gone dry and my knees were knocking as she pushed open the door to the mummy's tomb!

The Princess Of Porh

We stepped into the dim burial chamber. It was really eerie, lit only by a few of the ever-burning torches, and our elongated shadows flickered against the bare walls. The air was musty and chilly and in the middle of the room a high dais held an open, stone sarcophagus, heavily decorated with swirling carvings and inset with a myriad of gemstones. On one corner of the coffin stood a small onyx urn.

'Oh my goodness, this is really creepy,' whispered Philly as we crept to the edge of the coffin and peered in.

Lying on a bed of perfectly preserved purple satin was the dark, dry, mummified body of the long dead Purhian Princess Penelope.

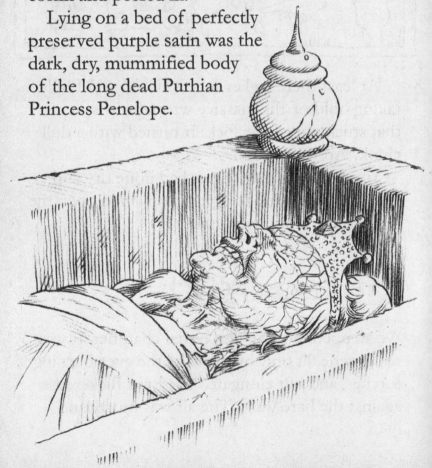

The skin of her sunken cheeks was as dry as parchment and covered with a network of tiny cracks; it looked so fragile that even a sneeze might break it up and send it fluttering across the room like autumn leaves blown from a tree.

On her thin wrists were half a dozen bangles of pure gold and on her head, flickering and sparkling in the light from the flames, sat the famous diamond tiara. Philly and I stared at each other in awe, hardly daring to breathe. Then, all of a sudden I felt something cold and clammy touch my leg.

'*Yikes!*' I screamed and leaped back from the coffin. What the heck was that? I looked down and there was Mad Dog, peering up at me with his lopsided grin.

'*Woof!*' He yapped, as if to say, *don't forget about me!* I burst out laughing and Philly and I breathed a sigh of relief. Our mechanical pooch had broken the awful tension in the burial chamber – there was nothing to be scared of here, no curses or spells or mythical monster guards!

'Let's get the tiara and get out of here,' I said and we both stepped back up to the coffin. I put my hand in, but somehow I couldn't take it. 'This doesn't seem right. You know, taking a precious jewel from the body of a dead princess.'

'Oh, whatever!' said Philly. 'She's been dead for centuries. If *you* can't do it, I can. If you think I've come all this way just to leave the tiara here *and* get Grandpa dropped into the barracuda tank as a result, you've got another think coming. It's a matter of life and death.' And she reached her hand into the coffin and lifted out the tiara!

Shafts of firelight, reflected from the burning torches, shot from the diamond-covered headband. As Philly turned the tiara in her hands, the beams played over the surface of the stone walls like lasers.

'See?' smiled Philly triumphantly. 'Nothing's happened.' But as she spoke, the onyx jar on the corner of the sarcophagus started to tremble. The vibrations grew stronger and stronger until the jar's lid started to rattle. All of a sudden the lid flew off and *WHOOSH!* a column of smoke poured up from the urn, coiling in the air and filling the room with a sweet, cloying scent like incense, that made my nose twitch and start to run.

The Smoke Demon ← Aaargh!

As the smoke billowed in the air, it started to form into a fearsome shape. I could make out a pair of evil-looking eyes and a long sharp nose with wide, quivering nostrils. It was a demon; an enormous demon made of smoke! Mad Dog started to bark. Gnashing his metallic teeth he hurled himself at the fiend – but charged right through the shifting wreaths of smoke; then, whimpering, sat down in confusion.

'Oh Charlie! Help!' cried Philly. 'What have I done?'

'Don't worry,' I stammered, although I was absolutely petrified of this looming, leering phantom. 'What can a smoke demon do? It can't bite us, and it can't scratch us with its talons. It's nothing but a scary picture!'

I was right; the demon couldn't bite, but as it coiled through the air, weaving itself between Philly and I, the air became nauseating and

thick. Heady aromas filled our lungs, making our heads spin. I felt faint, then sick and sleepy, and fell to my knees. I could feel myself tottering on the edge of consciousness and knew that if I lay down for just one second, I would be lost forever in a world of eternal sleep. Philly and I were being mummified!

Groggily, I groped around in my rucksack and found my trusty water bottle. Luckily it was full and, choking on the clouds of scented smoke, I unscrewed the cap. As the smoke demon coiled around my head once more and I felt my senses reeling, I swept the bottle in a wide arc through the air. Water sprayed out, hitting the sinister sprite in the face – and with horrible, eye-popping grimaces, it started to disintegrate! I sprayed some more at the demon and little wet droplets of smoke rained down, plopping on the floor. It was like watching a painting bleed.

The smoke demon started to disintegrate

As the last of the little smoky raindrops splashed to the floor, the atmosphere became clearer and Philly and I could breathe more easily. We took great gulps of air, trying to clear our heads. I got to my feet, helped Philly up and grabbed hold of Mad Dog's lead.

'Jeepers creepers, that was close,' I gasped.

'You can say that again,' puffed Philly. But as she said this, the little onyx urn began to rattle again and another column of smoke started to pour into the room.

'Run!' I yelled as a new demon started to form in the air above us and we ran out of the tomb and into the maze of corridors. Mad Dog pulled us along on the end of his lead.

We bolted along the passages, following our gnashing guide wherever he went, praying he was leading us the right way. Filling the corridor behind us came the billowing, grinning face of the new smoke demon. If we faltered or tripped, the demon would be upon us and we would quickly lose all our senses.

'Keep going!' I yelled. Then we were clattering up the stairs and along the huge hallway towards the main doors. As we ran out into the sunshine of the late afternoon with the demon hot on our heels, the wind grabbed hold of the smoky fiend, ripping it to raggedy shreds and lifting it high into the sky – where it disappeared like steam from a kettle.

We stopped, our chests heaving and our legs shaking.

'Come on, let's get back to the hover-sub while we're still in one piece,' said Philly when we'd got our breath back.

We crossed the great flat plateau and started to climb the jagged rocks up towards the gondola. But as we stepped onto the overhanging platform a noise from the lookout spire made us turn – uh-oh! Clattering down the steps came half a dozen animated skeletons, wielding their rusty swords!

'*Oh yikes!*' I cried. 'They must have come to life because we took the tiara. There *is* a curse on it! *Help!*'

We were trapped on the platform. The skeletons had cut off our route down to the plain and all we had behind us was the sheer drop to the rocks and the crashing waves below.

Attack Of The Skeletons

As the skeletons advanced, their bony feet clicking and clacking on the rock, we stepped back to the edge of the platform until we were teetering over the dizzying drop. I rummaged in my rucksack, desperately trying to find something that I could use as a weapon. My lasso! I pulled it out and span it around my head, once, twice and then let it go. The loop sailed through the air and came down over two of our skinny attackers. With a sharp yank I tried to pull them over the edge of the platform, but instead, with a clatter, the two skeletons simply fell apart and landed in a pile of old bones!

'*Yee-hah!*' I yodelled, and started to pull the lariat in, ready to make another attack. But one of the remaining bony buccaneers stepped forward and with a swish of his sword, sliced the loop right off my lasso!

Now we were in a real jam. There were four armed skeletons left, and apart from a one-inch penknife, there was nothing in my rucksack to defend myself with. (A glue pen or a set of collectors cards wouldn't have been much use.)

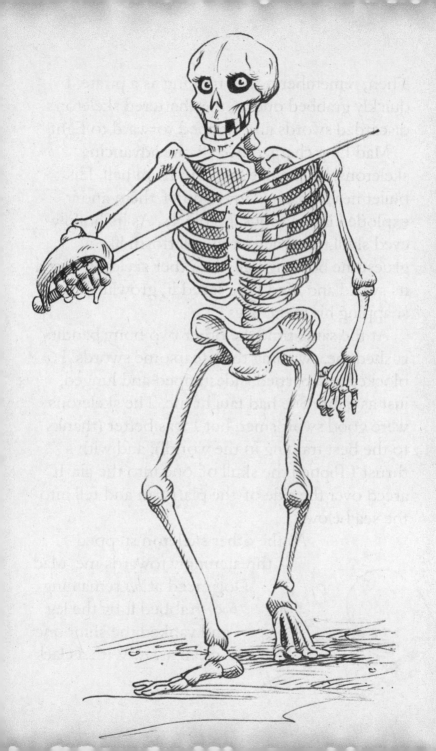

Then, remembering my training as a pirate, I quickly grabbed one of the shattered skeleton's discarded swords and stepped forward to fight.

Mad Dog charged two of the advancing skeletons, baying like a hound from hell. His bullet head smashed into one of them and it exploded into a thousand pieces. As its hollow-eyed skull rolled across the platform like a gruesome bowling ball, the other skeleton raised its sword and Mad Dog faced it, growling and snapping his metal jaws.

At the same time the other two bony bandits rushed me, swishing their fearsome swords. I blocked and parried, sidestepped and lunged, just as Sabre Sue had taught me. The skeletons were good swordsmen but I was better (thanks to the best training in the world!), and with a thrust I flipped the skull of one into the air. It arced over the side of the platform and fell into the sea below.

As the other skeleton stepped threateningly towards me, Mad Dog raced at *his* remaining foe, grabbed it by the leg and yanked the shinbone clean away. With a clack of surprise from its grinning jaw the skeleton collapsed and Mad Dog sat down, happily chewing on the ancient tibia. There were so many bones strewn about the mutt must have thought all his Christmases had come at once!

This wasn't helping me though. As I stepped back from my attacker, I tripped over a loose skull and crashed onto my back on the platform, my head hanging over the sheer drop. 'Help! Mad Dog, help me!' I yelled, but the mechanical mutt was too busy chewing on his treat. The skeleton loomed above me, raised his sword high and . . . *BOOF!* Philly flew at it with a flying rugby tackle and brought it crashing to the floor, where it lay motionless.

'Thanks, Philly,' I said, gasping for breath and scrambling to my feet. 'Everyone into the gondola.' I'd had quite enough of Purh Island!

We dived into the wooden cradle, lowered ourselves over the edge and slowly began to descend the cliff face. But halfway down I felt the rope start to judder violently and looked up to see that the last skeleton had come to life and was hacking away at the rope with its rusty sword.

'*No!*' I yelled, but it was already too late. With a loud *TWANG!* the rope snapped and we were tipped out of the gondola and dropping like stones towards the rocks below.

'*Help!*' Philly and I cried in terror – Mad Dog, though, was still happily chewing his bone as he fell!

'We're done for!' screamed Philly, just as I remembered my jetpack rucksack. I hoped it would still work after its dip in the sea.

I pressed the thruster button once, twice, three times and with a splutter the jets roared into life, instantly slowing my fall. Then, using the directional buttons I swooped down like Batman and grabbed Philly by the strap of her dungarees. Another boost of the jetpacks and

Philly was able to grab
Mad Dog by the collar and,
looking like some sort of aerial
display event gone wrong, we
descended safely to the jetty
at the base of the cliffs.
As the lone skeleton
bombarded us from above
with the bony remains of
his pals, I managed to grab
a skinny finger bone as proof
of my miraculous adventures
with the skeletal swordfighters.
See my sketch of the
disgusting digit!
With a cheeky wave to
the skeleton, I grabbed
my lasso from the rocks and
we all dived into the hover-sub.
Slamming the doors behind us,
Philly fired up the engines and
we roared out
to the safety of the open
ocean. *Yee-hah!*

Here is the finger bone I kept

Next stop Mayazapan

Both of us were exhausted after our terrible
battles on Purh Island – and I was famished.
What I needed was a fat fish finger sandwich,
covered in rich, gloopy tomato sauce! I put the
frying pan on to sizzle and Philly and I were
soon tucking into one of my favourite snacks.
Delicious!

Philly put the sub on autopilot and we
stretched out on our comfy chairs for the night.
Although the Chemical-powered Crustacean
Hover-sub is quite cramped inside, it is very
comfortable and has begun to feel like home.
Under the soft glow of the cabin lights and to
the comforting sound of little radar beeps from
the dashboard, I fell into a deep sleep.

I awoke, blurry-eyed, to find the late morning
sun streaming into our cockpit. We had driven
all through the night and now it is already the
third day of our mission. Time is getting tight
and we still have to pluck a spine from the back
of the world's last remaining golden porcupine!

Philly is at the controls of the hover-sub,
and I'm busy writing up this journal. The giant
pearl and the diamond tiara are safely secured

in one of the lockers, and Mad Dog is curled contentedly beneath my seat. The skeleton's shinbone is tucked under one of his metallic paws and his insides are making soft whirring and clicking noises.

The Land of Legends is full of the strangest animals I have ever seen. Right now there are two weird creatures less than ten metres away from our craft. As an explorer I must record them in my journal, and give them names:

The Helipuss: A sort of octopus that spins its tentacles so fast it can fly like a helicopter. It squirts its prey with ink as thick as tar, making it impossible for the poor thing to get away.

The helipuss

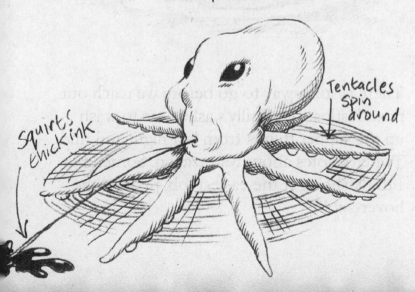

squirts
thick ink

Tentacles
spin
around

The Sea Potato: A large, shapeless mass that appears to be nothing but a mouth and stomach. All it does is float on the surface of the water, mouth open, waiting for its dinner to swim right in!

The Sea Potato!

dinner

There is still a way to go before we reach our next destination; Philly's asked me to wash up the supper things from last night and find Twitch's notes about Mayazapan. Sometimes I think she's got the easiest job, piloting the hover-sub!

Going Ashore

Now we are hiding on the white sands of a secluded beach, waiting for the sun to set.

Whilst Philly plotted our course and checked the instruments on the sub's dashboard, I had done all the washing up, swept the cockpit, oiled Mad Dog and made some sandwiches for our lunch; I was getting so bored of housework I was starting to look forward to a bit more danger and hoped we'd arrive at Mayazapan soon! It was late in the afternoon and I was studying Twitch's notes, when . . .

'*LAND AHOY!*' yelled Philly, nearly making me jump out of my skin. 'Is that Mayazapan?'

'Where?' I cried, and looking up saw a long grey smudge of land on the horizon.

As we got nearer we could see not one, but two separate islands, joined together by a precarious and narrow causeway. Clusters of dilapidated houses clung precariously to the steep sides of the larger island, like limpets on a rock. On the smaller island a tall, whitewashed wall ran along the entire length of the cliff tops. Above the wall poked domed and onion-shaped roofs, glittering with beautiful turquoise tiles. Just then the hooter sounded on our dashboard to announce we'd arrived at our destination.

'Yes, this is definitely Mayazapan. And I wonder which of the two islands the potentate lives on?' said Philly, sarcastically. 'The one covered in tumble-down shacks, or the one with the gleaming palace domes?' She turned the crustacean sub towards the smaller island.

'Be careful – we don't want to be spotted. It doesn't sound a very friendly place,' I said. 'Listen to this,' and I read her the notes left by Tristram Twitch:

Mayazapan is a mysterious country in the
Land of Legends, on the far side of the
wide and wild ocean. It is made up of two
islands connected by a rocky bridge. On the
larger island live the poor Mayazapanian
People. On the smaller one, in an extravagant
palace zoo, resides their leader, a cruel
and powerful potentate who loves
animals, but HATES PEOPLE'S GUTS!

The potentate spends all his wealth
on building a magnificent menagerie of
the most rare and exotic animals on earth.
It is one of the wonders of the world of
legends, but no one is allowed in the zoo
except the potentate himself and his scary
menagerie militia of simian servants
(chimpanzee guards to you and me! T.T.)
They are devoted to their leader and

cont:

defend the zoo with their very lives. It's no surprise that they're loyal; it is said that these chimps live a life of complete luxury and are given everything they desire.

Any visitors to Mayazapan must be very, very careful. It is rumoured that the few who have tried to take a peep inside the zoo were never heard of again. Be warned

Twitch

'Wow! You're right. We mustn't be spotted,' said Philly. 'It sounds as if this might be the trickiest task of all – and now we've only got forty-eight hours left to break into the palace zoo, find the golden porcupine and return to Tristram Twitch's warehouse hideout. Oh, brilliant!'

With a few adjustments to the instrument panel we dived under the waves, and went skimming along under the surface like a fat, prehistoric dolphin.

We skimmed beneath the surface towards Mayazapan

We emerged in a deserted bay on the potentate's menagerie island and with a quick thrust of the hover pads, drove up onto the pure white sands of the beach. Landing the sub behind a large, jutting rock for safety, we jumped down onto the seashore and looked up at the wall running along the headland.

'What shall we do?' asked Philly. Although it looked pretty deserted up there, we would be easily spotted if we tried to climb up from the bay.

'I vote we wait until nightfall,' I suggested. 'At least then we'll be able to sneak around the zoo without being seen. What do you say – if we manage to grab the golden quill tonight and then drive home at absolute full speed, will we be able to make it in time?'

'Just about,' said Philly, doing some quick calculations with her fingers. 'But we'll be cutting it really fine.' We decided to wait in the sub until dark.

Now the sun has set and it's time to start our mission. I've double-checked my rucksack and re-looped the lasso I'd managed to retrieve from the base of Purh cliffs. I have decided not to take my newly-won cutlass, as it might get in the way climbing up to the menagerie. Philly has refuelled the sub and oiled and tweaked the engine, ready for a quick getaway. Now she's standing by my side, her eyes shining with excitement and trepidation.

'Ready?' I asked.

'Ready,' Philly replied.

'Ruff,' yapped Mad Dog.

Oh boy, here we go . . . I'll write more just as soon as I can.

The Magnificent Menagerie Of Mayazapan

After the long clamber up from the bay in the moonlight, Philly, Mad Dog and I stood at the base of the tall white wall of the menagerie. All along the wall hung a row of warning signs.

'Yikes, have a read of that,' I said to Philly. The sign said:

> ABANDON HOPE ALL YE WHO ENTER HERE. THIS ZOO IS **PRIVATE**. ANYONE CAUGHT **TRESPASSING** WILL BE PUT IN THE MENAGERIE MINCING MACHINE AND FED TO THE ANIMALS. ❖ BY ORDER OF THE ❖ POTENTATE OF MAYAZAPAN

'What do you think?' I gulped.

'We haven't got much choice if we want to get a golden quill,' said Philly. 'Come on, Charlie, let's not give up now.'

The wall
was too
high for us
to climb,
even with a
leg-up – and
I didn't want to use my
jetpack rucksack in case it
made too much noise and
alerted the chimpanzee
guards. So, after tying a
series of knots along the
length of my lasso, I threw
the looped end over one
of the spikes sticking up
from the top of the wall.

Then, using the
knotted footholds,
we shinned up
the rope. I
had to carry
Mad Dog
and the silly hound didn't make
it easy, yapping and scrabbling his claws against
my chest.

'Shh, Mad Dog,' I whispered. 'You'll wake up

the whole zoo!' Even as I said this, we heard a low growl from the other side of the wall. Once on top, we dangled the lasso down the other side, slid to the ground and looked around.

'Wow!' said Philly softly. 'He must have every animal under the sun in here. How are we ever going to find the golden porcupine?' She was right. By the light of the moon we could see cages and animal houses spread out before us in every direction. Winding paths and shrub-lined walkways connected them all. The animal houses were painted white, had golden bars and were topped with ornate mosaic roofs. The paths were gravelled with marble pebbles, and wherever two paths crossed, there was a beautiful arched arbour.

'We'll just have to search until we find it,' I whispered. 'Now come on, and remember, not a sound.' I stepped onto the path and *CRUNCH!* the gravel sounded like fireworks going off under our shoes. 'Oh, brilliant!' I moaned. 'We'll have to go in our socks.'

Philly and I took our shoes off, tied the laces together and hung them round our necks. Then Philly took some oily rags from her dungarees and knotted them round Mad Dog's metal paws.

'That should do it,' she whispered as Mad Dog grinned inanely, and we set off again. Now we were much quieter and, luckily, the pebbles were so smooth they didn't hurt our feet. We crept along the edge of the path and past the first of the sleeping animals.

A Terrible Shock

The air was full of the grunts and growls of snoring beasts, and thick with the fusty, musty smell of straw and dung. I couldn't make out the first animal we passed; it was just an indistinct shape amongst the shadows at the back of the cage, but we could hear its steady, hoarse breathing. We could see the next animal, though: a magnificent tiger of awesome proportions that glowed like amber in the moonlight and had teeth the size of scythes. Mad Dog gave a quizzical whine.

'Be quiet,' I hissed and I stepped closer to the cage to read the sign:

THE SALAMANIAN SABRE-TOOTHED TIGER. ONLY FOUR OF THESE MAGNIFICENT BEASTS EXIST IN THE WILD. THEY CAN GROW TO THE SIZE OF A STALLION AND EAT 20 KILOS OF LIVE FLESH EVERY WEEK. IF YOU'RE READING THIS, YOU COULD BE NEXT WEEK'S MEAL.

As the animal snorted in its sleep, I stepped back in alarm.

'Let's go!' I whispered and we tiptoed down the path looking in every cage for the golden porcupine. We passed elephants with curved ivory tusks; two-headed tortoises with shells of burnished bronze and a silver-horned unicorn. It was very sad to see such magical beasts shut behind bars – even if they *were* bars of solid gold. If only I could free the poor things, I thought; but it would be silly to release a sabre-toothed tiger only to be gobbled up in one bite!

The two-headed tortoise

No, we had to concentrate on the task in hand.

Philly and Mad Dog and I sneaked up paths and along avenues and through animal houses full of sleeping, hissing emerald-green pythons and somnolent saw-toothed alligators, but we didn't see a golden porcupine anywhere.

Then, as we turned a shadowy corner, I got the shock of my life! Right in front of us was a menagerie guard: a steel-helmeted chimpanzee with long, powerful arms, carrying a heavy club. Luckily the chimp was sitting with its back to us and was busy grooming itself and picking its nose. We dived behind some shrubbery and waited for him to continue his round of inspection. As the powerful ape got to its feet and passed our hiding place, I realized just how big and strong it was. I knew if we were ever captured by one of these chimps, we wouldn't stand a chance.

'Come on, let's get a move on; if we're not careful we'll be running out of time,' whispered Philly. We carried on, hugging the dark borders and keeping a lookout for other chimp guards. Finally we stopped by a large cage, standing in deep shadow. We hadn't seen a single sign of a porcupine – gold, silver, or any other colour!

'It could

The chimpanzee guard

take us a year to find the stupid thing at this rate,' I said. 'I don't know what to do.' I crossed my arms and leaned back against the cage, feeling sulky. If I hadn't been in such a bad mood I would have known what a stupid thing it was to do. Before I knew what was happening, a thick hairy arm shot between the bars, grabbed me by the collar and lifted me clean off the ground!

'Charlie!' cried Philly.

'Shh!' I managed to croak as the hairy hand

turned me around and I found myself staring into the small angry red eyes of a massive silverback gorilla – and, oh yikes! It wasn't just any old gorilla!

Meeting An Old Enemy

'*THRAK!*' I gasped.

'*Uh, Ah!* You Charlie Small, jungle pest from Gorilla City,' he growled in the gutteral gorilla language I had learned when I was lost in the jungle.

Yes, it really was Thrak, the great gormless and aggressive ape I had met at the very start of my adventures, and he was obviously still peeved that I had beaten him in an arm wrestling contest to become king of the gorillas. In fact the last time I'd seen him, Thrak had swung me around his head and thrown me miles into the air. I had landed on Perfidy Island, home of Captain Cut-throat and her horrible gang of perfumed pirates. He was one of my worst ever enemies, so what he said next made me gasp with surprise.

'*Gnar!* Get me out of prison, Charlie. Please!' grunted the gormless gorilla.

'You've got to be joking!' I squeaked. I was sure he would rip my head straight off and use it as a basketball!

'Mean it, Charlie. I go mad in here. *Eee-eee, ah-ah-ah!*'

You were pretty mad to start with, I thought.

'What's going on, Charlie?' asked Philly. I realized she could only hear me and the gorilla exchanging guttural grunts.

'I'm talking gorilla,' I explained.

'Eh?' said Philly.

'Yap?' woofed Mad Dog.

'What are you doing here?' I grunted to Thrak.

'I was trapped in pit in jungle. Pit dug by potty potentate of Mayazapan. *Ooo-oo!* I fight, but they prick me with stick. I go to sleep. When I wake up, I in cage on boat. They bring me here. Two years ago. Get me out, Charlie, and we have a truce.'

'How do I know I can trust you?' I asked.

'I promise, Charlie,' pleaded the gorilla. 'If I want betray you, I call out now. Guards would come. Put you in mincer. I not do that.'

Thrak was very sad

'Do you know where the golden porcupine is kept?' I asked.

'*Gnnr!* Sure,' said the silverback. 'Get me out. I take you there.'

'But I don't know how,' I said. 'Look at the size of that lock.'

'Pick lock. You no got skeleton key?' said the gorilla, sighing like a deflating leather football.

'What's a skeleton key when it's at home?' I asked.

'Special key. Undo any lock; they used by burglars, bandits, spies. I thought you'd know that!' scoffed Thrak.

If only I still had that poisonous fish barb from the Copter fish that attacked me on board the *Betty Mae*, I thought. I'd used that as a key to help free Captain Cut-throat from pirate prison – but I hadn't seen it since. I'm pretty sure I dropped it when we hang-glided to freedom.

Then I had a flash of inspiration. 'OK,' I said to Thrak. 'Put me down. I've got an idea.' The gorilla lowered me to the ground. I opened my rucksack, switched on the wind-up torch (all mended since Mamuk had given me a new explorer's kit) and shone a beam over the contents. There – just what I was looking for! I picked up the skeleton's finger bone.

'What are you doing now?' asked Philly.

'Watch!' I said, and fed the long bony finger into the keyhole. I twisted and turned it, using all the skills I'd learned when practising to escape from the pirate's galleon. All of a sudden there was a dull click. Brilliant!

'You don't mean you're setting that hairy brute free?' squeaked Philly, and Mad Dog let out a little howl of fear as the cage door swung open and Thrak stepped out.

'Don't worry. I've had a word with him,' I said, repacking my rucksack. 'He's agreed to take us to the porcupine in return for his freedom.'

'If you say so,' said Philly, inching away from the massive monkey.

'Come; this way,' Thrak grunted. We followed his lumbering figure along the path.

The Golden Porcupine

Near Thrak's cage was a garden fountain
spraying coloured liquids high into the air, and
we followed the gorilla round the other side.
Here was a smaller cage, with the most ornate
roof and fancy metalwork of all.

'There,' grunted Thrak, pointing.

'That's the porcupine's cage?' I gasped
in disbelief. After all our efforts, we'd been
standing right next to the bloomin' thing! 'You
could have pointed this cage out to us.'

'*Ah, ooo!* But then I wouldn't be free, Charlie
Small,' said the gorilla and gave a great rumbling
chuckle.

You're not as daft as you look, I thought.

'Look, Charlie, isn't it wonderful?' whispered
Philly and I gazed between the bars of the
cage at what looked like a great clump of
yellow grass. All of a sudden, with a sound
like someone shaking a pencil case, the clump
moved. It was the golden porcupine shifting its
long spines.

Oh, wow! What an incredible creature.
Each spine was about a metre-and-a-half long
and made of solid, shining, polished gold.

The golden porcupine

They looked like a rack of the most expensive
javelins ever, glittering and gleaming in the soft
moonlight. With a sudden grunt, the animal
uncurled from sleep and raised its snub nose
in the air, sniffling and snuffling like a pig. The
porcupine must have picked up our scent, as
it shook and rattled its javelins in warning, but
then it curled into a ball and went straight back
to sleep, a handful of spines protruding through
the bars. All I had to do was reach over and
grab one – but I had a problem. Between the
cage and where we stood was a narrow, deep,
water-filled moat. And swimming in the moat
was a fat, wide-awake crocodile with a wide,
supercilious grin!

Getting A Lift

'How are we going to get over that?' asked
Philly. 'Have you got anything in your explorer's
kit that will help?'

I shook my head. 'Not that I can think of,'
I said. 'I might have been able to lasso a spine,
but I left my lariat dangling over the wall for a
quick getaway.' I looked to see if there was a
plank of wood or a ladder that had been left
lying around, but there was nothing. 'Any ideas?'
I grunted to Thrak.

WHOA! Without a word the mighty gorilla
picked me up. *No!* I thought. *The treacherous ape
is going to throw me to the crocodile!* But holding
me by my belt and one ankle, Thrak thrust me
across the gap towards the cage. The crocodile
popped its head above the water to take a look
and opened its jaws, waiting for me to drop.
*This must be how poor old Jakeman is feeling right now,
dangling above that barracuda pond,* I thought.

As Thrak held me over the moat, I gradually
started to bend down towards the crocodile's
gaping jaw. *Yikes!* I span my arms like a
windmill, trying to raise myself up. Just like this:

As I came up, I reached out to grab a spine, but the porcupine shifted and the spikes disappeared through the bars into the cage.

'Darn it, I can't reach!' I grunted. 'Can you move me forward a bit?'

Grabbing me by the seat of my jeans, Thrak stood on tiptoe right by the edge of the moat and held me out further. '*Gnnr!* Hurry up, Charlie. Getting cramp,' he grunted, and the crocodile cracked its jaws together in anticipation.

I threaded my arm carefully through the bars and my hand closed on a golden spine. Yes! I gave it a slight tug. Nothing happened. I tugged harder and still the thing didn't come loose. Then, getting a really firm grip, I gave an almighty yank and with a jolt the spine came flying out. The porcupine woke up with an ear-splitting squeal; my arm knocked against the bars and somewhere in the distance a siren went off! *Oh, blimey!*

Woo woo Woo!

Alarmed bars →

← *Golden spine*

As Thrak pulled me back to safety, the crocodile came shooting out of the water like a sea-to-air missile, and snapped. For a second I felt its warm breath on my face as it bit a chunk of hair from my fringe, before dropping back into the moat with a look of disgust and disappointment on its face.

'Let's go!' I cried as lights started to come on all over the zoo.

'*Mmn grrb!*' grunted Thrak.

'This way,' I interpreted for Philly and, as I tucked the unwieldy spine under my arm like a knight's lance, we raced after him. Yikes, this was going seriously wrong!

The Potentate Of Mayazapan!

As we sprinted down the marble path we could hear the cries of the chimp militia from the far end of the zoo. Animals were waking up all around us, screaming, chattering, roaring and neighing. It was sheer pandemonium!

All of a sudden the guard chimp we'd seen earlier dashed down a side path and blocked our way. He pulled his lips back in a screaming laugh and banged a vicious-looking club on the ground.

'*Ooo-ooo-ooo,*' the chimp yelled and charged straight towards us. Thrak stepped forward, grabbed the chimp by the scruff of the neck, span round and round like an olympic discus-thrower and launched the hapless ape into the air. It cartwheeled high over the cages and right over the wall. Thrak thumped his mighty chest and it boomed like a big bass drum.

'Nice one, Thrak,' I cried as we darted away at top speed.

All of a sudden we emerged into a wide, open space planted with ornamental trees. In the middle, chained to a tall, ornately carved pillar, was the most awesome animal I've ever seen.

'Oh my goodness,' gasped Philly, coming to a halt. 'Take a look at that, Charlie.'

It was a panther, as black as night, its muscles twitching beneath its sleek fur. The big cat slunk around the base of the column, roaring and spitting, its yellow eyes shining in anger and fear at the approaching commotion.

'Incredible!' I whispered, for from the panther's shoulder blades sprouted two enormous white wings, flapping in agitation. When the panther saw us, it lifted its head and gave a terrifying roar. Thrak responded with a roar of his own and thumped his chest. *BOOM, BOOM, BOOM!*

Thrak took a step towards the panther, and the animal crouched and spat again, extending and flexing its claws.

'No, Thrak,' I said. 'We haven't got time for your personal battles. The guards will be here soon . . .'

Just as I said this, a score of menacing monkeys came running into the open circle. Behind them swept a bony, angular human figure. His long, richly-coloured robes flapped behind him and his thin, bearded chin was thrust arrogantly forward. It was the Potentate of Mayazapan.

'Halt!' ordered the potentate in a loud and terrible voice, and the chimps immediately lined up around the edge of the piazza.

The mighty potentate took a step forward, his hand gripping a fancy staff. He looked for all the world like a magician from a pantomime.

The Potentate of Mayazapan

'You might as well give up, you know,' he said in a rasping, menacing tone. 'You don't stand a chance. Either way, you're going to end up in the menagerie mincing machine, so why not save yourself the humiliation of a fight and come quietly.'

'No way!' I yelled back.

'Yeah, no chance, buster,' said Philly.

'*Woof!*' barked Mad Dog in agreement.

'If that's the way you want it,' sighed the potentate. 'Troops, attention!'

The apes lifted their clubs.

'Ready!'

They took a step forward.

'Wait for it, wait for it, you 'orrible lot . . . Charge!'

Chimp Attack!

The chimps came speeding towards us. Oh heck!

'Philly, what shall we do?' I yelled. I could have used my jetpack rucksack to escape, but I couldn't leave Philly to bear the brunt of the attack on her own.

'I think we're going to get minced, Charlie!' she cried.

Then, with a loud bark, Mad Dog took off like a rocket. He hurtled towards the chimps, snapping his steel jaws!

'Go, Mad Dog, go!'

cheered Philly. Our mechanical canine friend crashed into the charging chimps, bowling the leading row to the ground like a set of skittles. A club was brought crashing down on his skull, but bounced off with no effect.

'Tempered steel plate,' explained Philly as Mad Dog clamped his jaws round the ankle of the offending chimp. The ape screamed in surprise. More blows rained down on Mad Dog and he made a tactical retreat, grinning like a fool. That dog sure loves a fight!

As the chimps advanced more cautiously towards us, I wielded the porcupine's golden spine like a spear, thrusting and jabbing and trying to fend them off. I glanced over my shoulder to see what Thrak was doing and was gobsmacked to see the stupid animal still roaring at the winged panther. As he lumbered towards the growling, slavering beast, I called out:

'Er, excuse me. If you wouldn't mind, we could do with some help here. Thrak! You useless twit!' But it was too late. The guards had surrounded us. One chimp grabbed me by the arm and prised the porcupine spine from my hand. Another leaped at Mad Dog and clamped a strong hand around his muzzle to stop him biting. Mad Dog growled and whined in frustration but couldn't shake himself free. Encircled by chimps, Philly and I were pushed and cajoled along the path to where the mighty potentate was waiting.

'No one enters my menagerie and lives to tell the tale,' he growled in a voice as rough as sandpaper. 'What is your business here?'

My captor handed him the golden quill and the potentate's eyes darkened with anger.

'So, not only are you trespassers, but also thieves,' he hissed. 'Your fate is sealed, you young fools. Chimps!' he screamed. 'Take these intruders straight to the mincing machine.' Then, to two of the largest chimps he bellowed, 'Go and grab that gormless gorilla and get him back in his cage.'

'Yes sir!' said the chimps with a smart salute, and started down the path.

As we were escorted away, I turned to look back at Thrak as the two chimps marched towards him. I expected to see him in mortal combat with the panther by now, but instead he was standing with the animal's chain stretched across his broad chest, pulling at the links with all the power in his thick arms. Oh wow! He

was trying to free the beast, not fight it!

Quick, Thrak, I thought, *hurry up. I don't know if you've got enough time!* Then our guards led us up a side path and the gorilla was lost from view.

The Menagerie Mincing Machine (yuk!)

At the end of a long path, built against one of the menagerie's walls, stood a machine about the size of a garage. There were pipes sprouting from every side; dials were turning and tubes squirted thick, pink gunk into large wheelie bins. The contraption was vibrating gently and emitting a continuous *gloppeta, gloppeta* noise.

'This is the zoo's food preparation unit,' hissed the potentate, pointing with the porcupine spine. 'Or the Gloppeta Gloppeta Machine as we call it. Perhaps you'd like to see how it works?'

Glopetta!

'Not especially,' said Philly.

'Oh don't be like that,' said the potentate,

with a menacing sneer. 'You'll be amazed at how efficient it is. There are lots of different grades of mincing the machine can perform for every size of animal in the zoo. Lion and tiger food doesn't need much preparation, whereas the fan-eared weasel and the star-nosed shrew require the finest of minced morsels. Very particular they are. Boris, please demonstrate.'

One of the chimps saluted the potentate and swung himself up a ladder onto the top of the mincing machine. He opened a hatch and a cloud of chilled air escaped from within. It was some sort of fridge and, reaching down inside, the chimp pulled out half a carcass of beef. Swinging it over his shoulder, the ape dropped the carcass into a wide metal hopper, pulled a lever and the carcass dropped inside. *Gloppeta, gloppeta, gloppeta* went the machine.

I gulped, because I knew this was where Philly and I were going to end up unless something truly miraculous happened. As my mind swirled with a hundred possibilities, none of them good, I heard a faint yell and looking up into the night sky, saw the tiny silhouette of a chimp cartwheeling through the air. It disappeared over the wall and dropped towards the sea. A second later another chimp followed the same route. No one else seemed to notice. *Good old Thrak*, I thought, *he's beating them.*

A loud grinding noise brought me to my senses. The machine began to rock, the dials started to spin and a shrill whistle sang. Neatly butchered chunks and joints began to emerge from one of the tubes at the bottom of the machine and drop into a bin, around which a swarm of fat flies were buzzing.

'Specially graded for the big game,' smiled the potentate. 'Now watch.' He turned a dial and immediately the machine's grinding noise became a hum. A fine, pink minced paste oozed from one of the other tubes. 'That's for the little'uns and I think we'll keep it on that setting for you two. The metal dog, I'm afraid will have to be disposed of another way!'

Mad Dog tried to bark angrily but a chimp still had his muzzle clamped shut.

'Now, who's first?' asked the potentate, rubbing his long-fingered hands together. Strangely enough, neither Philly nor I volunteered. 'The girl, then: Boris, mince 'er!' Boris reached down one of his strong, hairy arms and pulled Philly kicking and yelling onto

the mincing-machine
roof.

'No!' I bellowed.
'Leave her alone.'

'Or what?' sneered the
potentate as Boris lifted
Philly over the gaping
mouth of the hopper.
'Drop her in, Boris. Hee,
hee, hee,' he ordered,
with a grating chuckle.

'*Ooo, oo, oo!*'
screeched Boris,
grinning
grotesquely as
he held the kicking
girl high above his head. *Help!*

Drop her in, Boris!

Thrak To The Rescue!

A terrifying roar sounded from behind and we
all turned to see Thrak standing at the top of
the path. With a mighty thumping of his chest
he swung his arms and bared his khaki teeth.

'Get him!' ordered the potentate, and the

remaining chimps formed a line and attacked. *BOOF! BASH! BIF!* Thrak waded amongst them, swatting chimps to the left and right as if they were nothing more than stalks of grass.

And then, all of a sudden, *WHOOSH!* a coal-black shape swooped from the sky, grabbed Philly from Boris the ape's hands, and carried her up into the air. It was Thrak's friend, the winged panther!

'Who freed Simbah?' screamed the potentate as the big cat swept across the night sky. With a flick of its wings, the panther came racing back towards us, Philly dangling from its claws. The cat flew down the path and in one fluid movement placed Philly gently on the ground, curled its claws around the collar of the potentate's robes and rose into the sky again.

'No, Simbah, no!' squealed the petrified potentate, dropping the golden spine as he struggled to free himself from the panther's claws. 'Put me down. Put me down . . .' But the potentate's voice grew fainter and fainter as the winged beast disappeared over the wall and off across the moon-flecked ocean.

'*Aaah, aah!*' screamed the few remaining chimps. Speaking fluent gorilla I knew the terrified screams meant: 'Retreat, retreat. The master is gone!' As one, they scattered, legging it down the zoo's manicured paths and leaping over the perimeter wall.

'Well done, Thrak! You saved us,' I cried, panting with fear and excitement as I retrieved the discarded golden porcupine spine.

The panther swooped out of the sky

'We had bargain, Charlie. You helped me, I helped you,' he grunted.

'Where has Simbah gone?'

'He gone home,' said Thrak. 'Long, long way – but taken lunch with him. *Ooo, eee, aah!*'

As Philly and I knelt down to put our shoes back on, the sun started to rise above the horizon, bathing the zoo in a warm, golden glow.

'Oh yikes! We'd better get going, Philly. We've got to be home by tonight!' I said. But then a whimper sounded from one of the nearby cages. It was a strange-looking dog – a Pamovian hunting dog. Philly looked questioningly at me.

'What are we going to do about all these poor animals?' she asked. 'We can't just leave them here. There's no one to feed them now.'

'*We* can't stay, Philly,' I said. 'Perhaps Thrak could look after them.'

'Uh?' exclaimed Thrak with a look of horror on his face.

'Oh Charlie. We can't leave poor Thrak here; not after all he's done for us. Couldn't we drop him off at a jungle island or something, on our way home?'

She was right of course. Thrak deserved to be returned to the wild. 'Would you like that?' I asked him, translating what Philly had said.

'Back to real jungle?' growled Thrak. '*Ooo, oo,* Yes! Any jungle will do, *ooo, ooo!*'

'OK,' I said to Philly. 'But that doesn't solve the problem of the other animals. What about the people of Mayazapan – the ones on the other island? Do you think they would help?'

'Maybe,' said Philly. 'But what if they are just like their potentate?'

'*Gnar, gnash, oo-ah!*' rumbled Thrak, meaning, 'People of Mayazapan hate potentate. He spend all money on zoo and keep them poor. They help.'

'But we can't hang around to ask them,' I said. 'We've got to go now, or we won't get back in time to save Jakeman. What shall we do?'

'Gnar! Write letter,' said Thrak. 'I give to Pamovian dog. He take to villagers on big island.'

'Good thinking, Thrak,' said Philly, once I'd translated his idea to her. 'Have we got any paper?'

I tore a sheet of paper from this notebook and handed it to Philly. This is what she wrote:

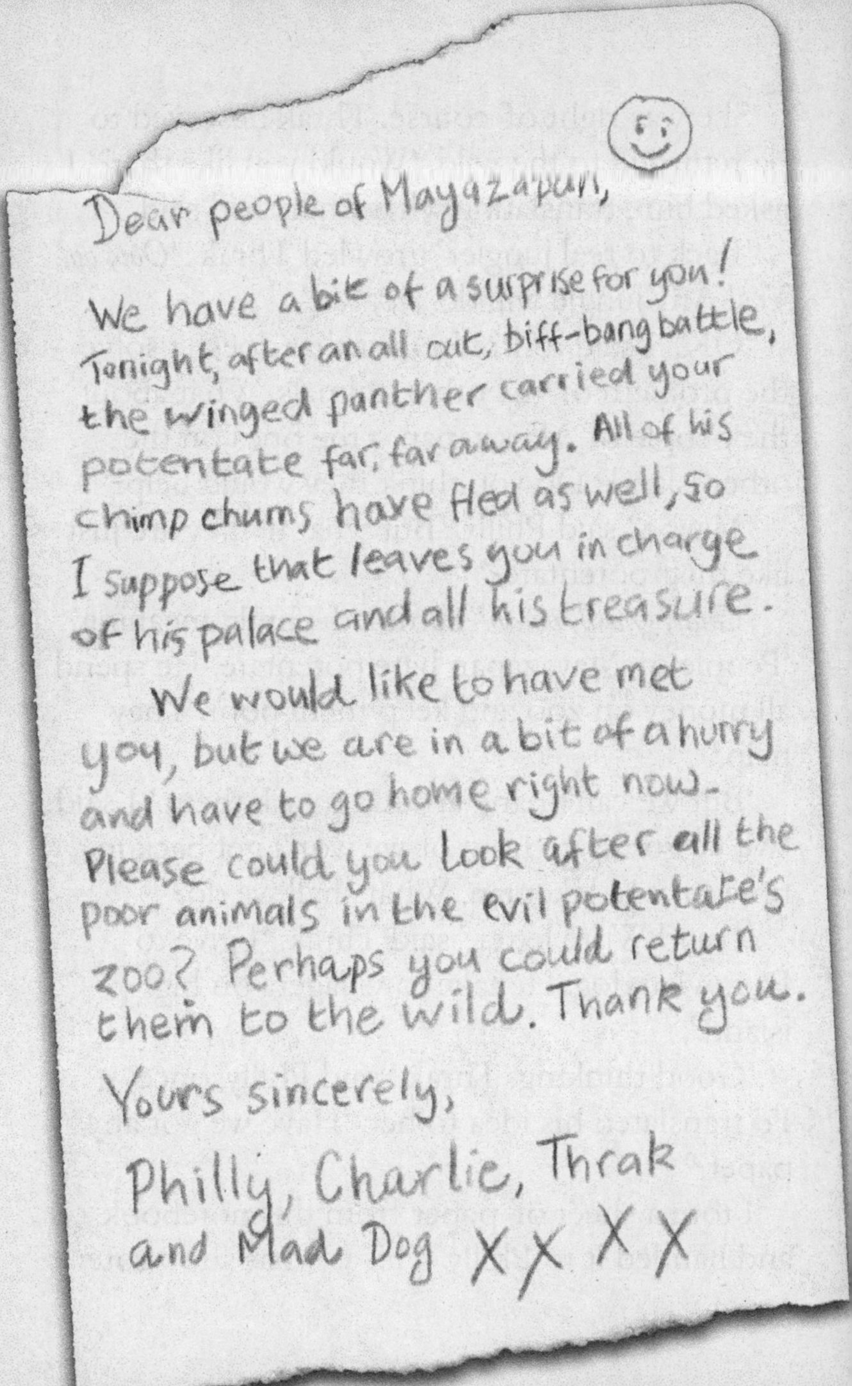

Dear people of Mayazapan,

We have a bit of a surprise for you!
Tonight, after an all out, biff-bang battle,
the winged panther carried your
potentate far, far away. All of his
chimp chums have fled as well, so
I suppose that leaves you in charge
of his palace and all his treasure.

We would like to have met
you, but we are in a bit of a hurry
and have to go home right now.
Please could you look after all the
poor animals in the evil potentate's
zoo? Perhaps you could return
them to the wild. Thank you.

Yours sincerely,

Philly, Charlie, Thrak
and Mad Dog X X X X

'That should do it,' said Philly, handing the letter to Thrak. With a terrific grunt, he heaved at the bars on the Pamovian dog's cage. They started to buckle and bend and the dog slipped through and jumped down onto the path.

'*Gnarr, ruh, ma ne nog!*' grunted Thrak to the animal as he bent down and fastened the letter to its collar.

'*Aaoooow!*' The dog threw back its head, howled at the sky and raced off down the path towards the potentate's palace.

'You can speak Pamovian dog talk?' I asked, astounded.

'International animal talk we develop in zoo,' said Thrak. 'He gone to deliver letter to people. Can get out through palace window.'

'Brilliant,' cried Philly. 'What are we waiting for, then? Let's go!'

Homeward Bound

We retraced our steps over the menagerie wall, where I retrieved my precious lasso, and headed down to the bay where the hover-sub was waiting.

There was a bit of a problem when we tried to board the sub, because, try as we might, Thrak just wouldn't fit in. His great powerful shoulders were too wide to squeeze through the narrow airlock door.

'What are we going to do?' asked Philly.

'Don't leave me here,' begged Thrak. 'Want to go to nice lush jungle. Want to climb canopy of rainforest; meet other gorillas. I've changed, Charlie. Will never be bully again.'

I scratched my head. How on earth could we transport the humungous great ape across the ocean? Then I had a brilliant idea.

'I've got it,' I said. 'How good are you at balancing, Thrak?'

'Balancing? Well, can balance one-legged on thin branch at top of tallest tree in jungle. Is good enough?'

'That should do it,' I said and went over to where I'd spied some driftwood lying on the shoreline.

'What are you up to?' asked Philly as I returned with a storm-battered plank. 'Wait and see,' I said.

I tied my lasso to two big bolts on the tail of the hover-sub. Thrak stood on the plank and held on tight to the lasso. As I climbed aboard the sub,

I shouted to Philly to start up the engine.

'Are you ready?' I called out from inside, over the loudspeaker system. Thrak, eyes wide with panic, nodded his head nervously. 'Go!' I said to Philly and she pushed the joystick forward. The hover-sub roared away, throwing up a big wave of water that came crashing down on Thrak's head. Whoops! Craning my neck I could just make Thrak out as he was jerked forward on his homemade water-ski with a force that would have pulled anybody else's arms from their sockets! Wobbling like a jelly, he was dragged along behind us, roaring at the top of his voice!

We could hear Thrak's screams and yells for quite a while as we blasted over the ocean.

'*Gnar!* I get you for this, Charlie Small,' he bellowed but, after a while, his complaints stopped and from what I could see of him, he seemed to be quite enjoying himself. In fact I got the distinct impression he was even doing some fancy tricks, skiing first on one foot and then on the other; he tried it one-handed and even, for a while, a bit of very impressive backwards water-skiing! Who would have thought a silverback gorilla would enjoy water sports so much?

Cheerio Thrak

We couldn't risk taking Thrak across the Great Divide, so we stopped at the first tree-covered island we spotted.

'You great, useless, brainless, pink potato-head,' yelled Thrak as we pulled him to a gradual stop in a wide, turquoise cove. Above the bay loomed a tall mountain covered in thick jungle that spread right down to the edge of the golden sands. It was an idyllic spot.

Thrak, though, wasn't in a very good mood.

'Why, what's wrong?' I asked. 'Look at that

Thrak's Island

forest! I thought you'd be pleased.'

'I mean water-skiing, you twit. I nearly broke neck. Stupid idea, dragging me behind super-speedboat.'

'Well,' I said, feeling quite shocked. 'It worked, didn't it? Here you are at a beautiful jungle. Anyway, we thought you did really well. We were very impressed with your tricks, weren't we?' I said, turning to Philly.

'Oh, absolutely,' said Philly and sniggered. Mad Dog yapped.

'Tricks? TRICKS? I wasn't doing tricks, you nit. I hanging on for dear life. *Gnar!*' With that, the angry gorilla paddled off through the shallow water towards the beach. Turning round and banging his chest loudly three times, he shouted out, 'And our truce over. If I see you again, Charlie, it's all-out war!'

'Oops,' I said to Philly as she started up the engines once more. 'I think we may have annoyed him a bit.'

'I think you're right,' she said. 'But he did look funny, zooming along on one leg!' And we both burst out laughing while Mad Dog tore around the cabin, barking at the top of his mechanical voice.

We raced home at top speed; we only had until sunset or we would fail in our task and Jakeman would be used as barracuda bait. As Philly manned the controls, I added the porcupine quill to our hoard. I couldn't believe it. We had managed to get all of Tristram Twitch's gifts for his beloved Aveline. They *were* beautiful and it was a shame they were going to such an awfully spoiled brat.

Before long, we reached the Great Divide once again. We disappeared into the huge swirling cloud and were soon being thrown about by the terrible currents. This time, though, Philly expertly steered our craft around the rim of the wicked whirlpool and although we were sent spinning round and round like a top, she managed to avoid getting sucked into the vicious vortex of water. Battered and scratched, the hover-sub emerged from the fog and we set our course for Twitch's warehouse.

As we sped over the ocean I brought my journal right up to date. It's been a fantastic adventure, I must say, but I do hope there are no other surprises. I'll let you know just as soon as I can . . .

The Deserted Warehouse

Finally, Philly steered the craft down the little canal that led into the warehouse. We were late, we knew we were; the sun had set and thousands of stars were already twinkling in the black sky.

'Oh, I hope Twitch will give us a bit of leeway,' cried Philly, a look of worry on her freckled face as we climbed out of the sub, ran across the plank and leaped onto the cobbled floor. Mad Dog trotted behind us.

The warehouse was in darkness and, apart from the muffled singing from the Black Swan across the yard, it sounded very quiet. *Oh no*, I thought, *we're too late after all.*

'Maybe they're upstairs waiting for us,' said Philly, and by the dim light coming through the grimy windows from the sailor's pub, we climbed the wooden staircase. This room was in darkness as well, and our hearts sank. The packing cases and spice barrels were piled up against the walls; Tristram Twitch's sofa still stood at the end of the room; but there was no sign of the fussy, twittering man or his two gormless minders, Syd and Perce.

'I don't believe it; they've gone. We've failed, Charlie. And that means Grandpa . . .' Philly's voice faded into silence as we stared at each other in horror.

'Don't give up hope, Philly,' I cried, grabbing her hand and racing up the flight of stairs to the room where Twitch's contraption stood. Up by the rafters flapped the sack, empty of all its grain. I gulped. This didn't look good. I rushed over to the loading doors and looked down to where the rope disappeared into the tank below.

The bag of grain was completely empty— Oh no!

'Well?' asked Philly, too nervous to look. Mad Dog gave a little whimper.

'I don't know. Give me a hand to pull the lobster pot up.'

We grabbed the rope that dangled down from the ceiling and pulled and pulled and pulled. With a splash, the lobster pot lifted from the tank. Pouring rivulets of water, the pot rose up the outside of the wall until it was level with the loading-bay platform. I tied the end of the rope to a big metal ring in the warehouse floor and then ran over and hauled the pot in through the doors.

A hole the size of a football had been ripped from one side of the basket, and inside we could see a little pile of bones that had been picked completely clean.

'No – Grandpa!' yelled Philly, and collapsed in a heap on the floor.

'Hold on! They're not human bones,' I cried. 'They're chicken bones. It's the remains of Jakeman's dinner, not him!'

'Are you sure?' asked Philly.

'Sure I'm sure. Look, here's the wishbone!'

'Where is he then?' cried Philly. 'What's

Twitch done with my grandpa?'

'Oh don't carry on so,' said a high voice from behind us. 'Jakeman is quite safe!'

Twitch Turns Up (like a bad penny!)

We span around and there, at the top of the steps, stood Tristram Twitch, Syd and Perce. Mad Dog growled so hard at the sight of these ominous-looking strangers, his whole body shook.

'Where is he?' demanded Philly.

'Can't you turn that manic mutt off or something?' stuttered Twitch, looking slightly alarmed at the shuddering Mad Dog. 'He's giving me the willies!'

'He's all right. He won't attack unless we tell him to,' I said.

'I asked what you've done with my grandpa,' demanded Philly.

'We let him go. He's back at his factory, if you must know,' said Twitch, trying to appear nonchalant as Mad Dog growled again.

'I knew you were bluffing. I knew you wouldn't really let Jakeman be devoured by a

170

ravenous barracuda,' I said.

'Oh, we tried, believe me,' said Twitch with a sigh. 'But he kept escaping! I don't know how he did it, but he managed to squeeze out of the little hole in the top of the lobster pot. It's meant to be impossible, and try as we might, we couldn't work out how he did it; the first two mornings we found him sitting up here waiting for us!'

'Good old Grandpa,' cried Philly. 'He's much too clever for the likes of you.'

'I'll ignore that remark,' sniffed Tristram Twitch. 'Anyway, he was proving to be more trouble than he was worth, so in the end we gave up and let him go back to his factory. After all, you were already on your mission and couldn't know Jakeman was free. So it wasn't going to affect my plans. You'd still be trying your darnedest to get the gifts and return in time to save him.' Then with his big eyes flashing with sudden greed, he added, 'Talking about your mission – did you manage to get my three lovely baubles?'

'What if we did?' I asked. 'Now that we know Jakeman is safe, we don't have to give them to you.'

'Oh Charlie, Charlie, Charlie,' twittered Twitch. 'I'm a little disappointed in you. I need my priceless pressies more than ever now; do you really think I will let them slip so easily from my grasp? Grab them, boys!'

As Syd and Perce lumbered forward, Philly cried, 'Get 'em, Mad Dog!' Twitch retreated nervously behind a pile of empty sacks, staring as the furious dog attacked his two thugs. Before they knew what was happening, Mad Dog had leaped at Syd and sunk his teeth into his big, fleshy bottom.

'*Yeow!*' screamed Syd, trying to prise the dog's jaws apart. 'Get this thing off me, Perce!'

'Sorted!' cried Perce, taking a run up and aiming a massive kick at our dangling dog. Mad Dog wasn't stupid, though, and as Perce swung his heavy boot, the dog let go of

Syd's bum and dropped to the floor. Perce's kick connected with Syd's already bruised rear.

'*Yeow!*' Syd bellowed again and went sprawling to the floor. The huge man landed with a crash right on top of Mad Dog, pinning him to the ground.

'Bung us a sack!' yelled Syd.

Twitch flipped an empty sack from the top of the pile in front of him. In one swift movement, Syd opened the mouth of the sack, pushed the confused canine inside and tied a double knot in the end. He stood up, triumphantly holding out the wriggling sack. 'That's enough of him,' he grinned, and dangling the bag over the stairwell, dropped it to the floor below. 'And now for you two!' he said to Philly and me. 'Come on, Perce, let's nab 'em.'

Philly and I darted across to the other side of the room, weaving between the wooden pillars and leaping over coils of rope. Syd lunged at me, his thick arms wrapping around my shoulders.

'Got you, you little devil,' he cried, but with a

well-aimed kick to his legs, I slithered out of his grip and he bent to rub his bruised shins.

'Oh, not again,' he wailed. 'Wait until I get my 'ands on you!'

Philly was hiding behind one of the thick pillars, dodging first one way and then the other as Perce tried to grab her from the other side.

'Stand still, you little worm,' he yelled.

Looking across the room, I noticed that Twitch was no longer anywhere to be seen and the way to the top of the stairs was clear. Had he run away in fear, or had he gone down to search the hover-sub for the booty? I didn't mind – we had an escape route.

'Run for it!' I yelled to Philly, and we both rushed towards the staircase. But as I reached the top step, Twitch stepped out from behind a tall stack of packing cases where he'd been hiding.

'I think it would be best for you if you stopped right there, Charlie,' he said, and hearing a click I span around to find he had a tiny engraved silver pistol pointed right at me. I froze on the spot.

'I hate to resort to such violence, but you've given me no choice. This might look like a toy,' said Tristram Twitch with one of his sweetest and most innocent smiles, 'but it could blow a hole right through the warehouse wall. So, if you want to keep your head on your shoulders, do exactly as I say.'

Syd and Perce grabbed us by our collars, and with Twitch still pointing the pistol, marched us downstairs, passing a growling and wriggling sack on the way.

What Happened To Aveline?

'Now, there's no need for us to fall out any more, Charlie,' said Twitch. 'So I'll ask you once again. Did you cross the Great Divide – and did you complete the three tasks?'

'Yes,' I sighed. 'We got your wedding gifts, you dandified dolt. So you can go to Aveline and tell her what a brave and heroic adventurer you are.'

'Aveline? That treacherous turncoat?' cried Twitch. 'She's not getting her hands on them.'

'But I thought you needed them in order to marry her?' I said.

'And so I did,' sighed Twitch, with a slight sniff as his large eyes filled with tears. 'I've had a very near escape, Charlie. Read this,' he said, handing Philly a letter and mopping his brow dramatically with his hanky. 'It came yesterday morning.'

Philly read out loud:

Oh my goodness. It's got to be the Perfumed Pirates. So they had been around after all!

Dear Tristram,

I know you are away, busy risking life and limb to get my wedding presents (and I know I'm worth it). But, if you do make it home I'm afraid I won't be here to welcome you. Sorry, and all that, but people change - and I've had a change of mind.

Oh, what a difference a day can make. Only yesterday morning I was so eager to get my wonderful gifts (and to see you, of course) that I went down to the docks to ask if there was any news of your expedition - but nobody seemed to know anything about it. That was strange, I thought. What was even stranger was that, when I happened to glance up at a window in a horrible old warehouse, I'm sure I saw you standing there, looking out to sea. But it couldn't have been you, could it? You are still away on your adventures. Silly old me!

Anyway, when I was there I bumped into the sweetest group of ladies you could ever meet. They said they came from a place called Perfidy, and they were very interested in the tales I had to tell them of all the treasures that lay beyond the Great Divide.

They asked me why I'd be happy with just a few trinkets when they could get me a whole house full of treasures? They promised to take me to the Land of Legends in their galleon, if I could supply them with all the maps and stuff that you traced from my ancient copy of the explorer's logbook. You must admit, Tristram darling, it does make sense! And who knows; If I'm lucky I might be able to win the hand of that mega-rich Potentate of Mayazapan. After all, how could he resist me?

So, I'm off. Don't expect me back. I'm sure I'll be married to the richest man in the Land of Legends before the week is out! And don't be upset. I'm sure you'll meet someone else - though not as beautiful as me, of course.

Wish me luck, Aveline

No way! He'll be stewing in the winged panther's stomach!

'Can you believe it?' gasped Twitch. 'Turned down at the last minute!'

'Oh dear! I'm so sorry about that,' said Philly, looking very concerned. 'It must have been a great shock.'

'Thank you, m'dear,' said Twitch, with a sniff and a wistful look in his eye. 'It was a terrible shock. All my expectations of a life of leisure and riches come to nothing.'

'Hold on,' I said to Philly. 'How can you feel sorry for a man who kidnapped me, dangled your Grandpa over a man-eating fish bowl and has a silver pistol pointed at us? I mean, really!'

'I was being sarcastic,' said Philly. 'Of course I don't care that this puffed-up peacock isn't going to marry his Aveline. Although they sound perfectly suited to each other. They're both spoiled, selfish, slimy and stupid.'

'I say, steady on,' cried Twitch, looking shocked. 'I'm not all that bad, y'know. I mean, everyone wants a bit of treasure to stash away, don't they?'

'No,' said Philly. 'Not if it means using an old man as barracuda bait.'

'Well, I'm sorry you feel like that,' said Twitch. 'I've never meant you any real harm, y'know.'

I exploded. 'Didn't mean us any harm? You've just sent us on a mission so dangerous you were too scared to go yourself, you fathead,' I yelled. 'We were nearly crushed by oysters, asphyxiated by smoke demons and minced in an industrial meat-mincing machine.'

'Oh don't exaggerate, Charlie,' sighed our foppish captor. 'I haven't got time to argue with you. Where's my treasure? Now I'm not marrying Aveline I need all the dosh I can get.'

'It's in the hover-sub,' said Philly.

'Off you go then,' said Twitch, waving his gun towards our boat. 'And quick about it.'

Philly started down the gangplank, but just then there was a loud knocking on one of the sliding doors.

'Open up, Twitch!' said a deep voice. 'We know you're in there!'

Twitch Makes A Run For It!

Twitch turned as white as a ghost and his little silver pistol dropped from his shaking hand, bounced on the floor and plopped into the canal!

'Bloomin' 'eck, boss!' cried Syd. 'It's the customs men. Let's get out of here!'

'The customs men – what do they want?' I asked.

'Just a little matter of some harmless smuggling . . . I thought I'd given 'em the slip but, oh my lord, they've tracked me down! If we're caught it means a ten-stretch in the clink! You'll have to take us out in your hover-sub, Philly.'

'There's no way you'll all fit in there,' said Philly. 'It was cramped with just the two of us.'

'Just take me then,' cried Twitch. 'These two can fend for themselves – aargh!' Syd had grabbed Twitch by his lacy collar, lifted him from the floor and with a squeeze of his massive hand started to throttle the floundering fop! 'You ain't goin' anywhere without us, boss,' he growled.

'But Syd, I've got nothing to offer you now,' croaked Twitch, starting to turn purple in the face. 'Let's go our separate ways.'

'You still owe us six months' wages, you scented scoundrel, and sooner or later you're gonna pay up,' snarled Syd. 'And if you're nabbed, I wouldn't put it past you to turn Queen's evidence and land me and Perce right in it, in order to save your own skin, you weasel.'

'OK! OK! We'll stick together,' wheezed Twitch. 'Now, please let go!'

Syd released his grip and Twitch dropped to the floor, gasping for breath.

There was a tremendous crash at the door.

'They've got a battering ram. They're goin' to smash it down!' said Perce, peeping out onto the yard from a filthy window. 'Let's go, Syd.'

As the two goons scrambled up the stairs dragging a reluctant Twitch behind them, Philly darted across the room, picked up the sack containing our furious pooch, and we raced for the hover-sub. We were desperate to put as much distance as we could between Twitch's gang and us as quickly as possible! I slammed the hover-sub hatch closed and Philly started up the engine; then, ignoring the speed limit, we flew along the canal.

When we passed under the arched exit, I saw the beleaguered door finally give way. It exploded in a thousand splinters and a group of men raced into the warehouse. They immediately clambered up the stairs after Twitch and his chums. Ha-ha, good riddance to bad rubbish!

Philly and I sped out into the moonlit harbour and I was finally able to let poor old Mad Dog out of his sack. He shook himself and woofed importantly, trying to regain some of his lost dignity, and then spoilt the impression

by giving us one of his idiotic grins! Philly
laughed, turning the sub towards the opposite
headland – and Jakeman's factory. *Yee-hah!*

Jakeman's Factory At Last! – Yippee!

'Phew! That was a close call. What a two-faced,
snivelling wretch Twitch is!' I said, as Philly
steered across the estuary of the wide river. 'Do
you think they got away?'

'I hope not,' said Philly. 'I hope
the customs men got them – or
they fell in the barracuda tank
when they tried to leap over
it! Not that Twitch would
be very easy to digest. Poor
fish would probably get
tummy ache!'

As we reached the far
side of the estuary, Philly
drove the sub between
outcrops of tall, sharp
rocks and tied up at a
little hidden platform carved
into the cliff face. Gathering

A Barracuda with tummy ache!

184

my explorer's kit, the canvas bag containing the pearl and tiara, and tucking the golden porcupine quill under my arm, I followed her up a flight of stone steps that had also been hewn out of the rock face.

It was a long climb and I was soon puffing and gasping for air. It was worth the hike though because when I got to the top, the most wonderful sight met me. Straight ahead was Jakeman's factory; the place I had been heading for ever since I met the inventor at the Battle of the Wasteland in the Wild West.

(See my Journal Destiny Mountain)

Row upon row and floor upon floor of grimy windows shone out into the dark; soot-blackened chimneys disappeared into a layer of coal smoke; the yard was littered with pieces of engine and crankshafts, rusted steel plates from the sides of battleships and old, spoke-less pram wheels. It was the most beautiful sight in the world!

Dear Old Jakeman

We walked under an arched sign painted with the legend *Jakeman's Works*, and Philly led me into the factory through a big sliding door that stood slightly open. I slid off my rucksack, put down the heavy treasure bag and spine and had a look around. The place was amazing; every available inch was taken up with steam-hammers, mechanical drills, lathes and a hundred complicated contraptions I couldn't guess the purpose of.

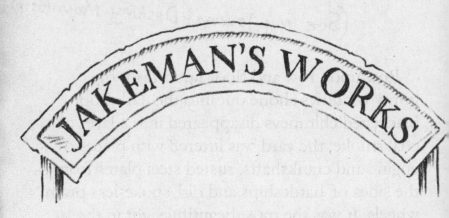

Chains hung from rails that ran overhead; a row of boilers lined the far side, glowing with heat, and along one of the walls stood a bank of computers. Their screens beeped and flashed up a constant stream of numbers. Jakeman was standing with his back to us, turning a piece of metal on a lathe.

'Hi, Grandpa,' said Philly, and Jakeman span around and beamed.

'Philly! Charlie! You're back safe and sound,' he cried, running over and giving Philly a huge hug, spinning her round and round. 'And Mad Dog too!' he beamed, as the mechanical mutt jumped up at the inventor, wagging his little metal tail. 'Where on earth did you find him?'

'We found him on the Island of Purh,' grinned Philly. 'But all of that can wait. How are you, Grandpa? We hear that Tristram Twitch and his pals couldn't keep you in the lobster pot!'

'No way!' chuckled the old man. 'What they didn't know was that as a young man I trained as an escapologist in a circus! There was no way a silly old lobster pot could hold the Great Jakinski! There's not a lock in the world that could hold me.'

'Except that locked door in the Underworld when the Shadow held you prisoner,' I reminded him.

'Ah, well yes,' blustered the old inventor. 'That

THE GREAT JAKINSKI

Gasp as Jakin escapes from inside a locked trunk, dangling from a bridge

was a bit different. That was a very ancient and particularly complicated device. But I'm sure I would have solved it eventually. Now, um, that's enough about me. How did your mega, mind-blowing mission go – and where is that great twit, Twitch?'

'Oh, we succeeded, Grandpa. We completed all the tasks. When we got back Twitch was waiting for us, but before we could give him his gifts the customs and excise men came looking for him. He had to do a runner – and he left his plunder behind!'

'Well I never. How wonderful – I suppose I can stop working on this now,' he said, pointing to the pile of pistons and tubes he'd been turning on the lathe. 'I was busy building another hover-sub in case I had to come and rescue you. I should have known I wouldn't need it with two intrepid swashbucklers like you. Come on – I want to hear all about your adventures!'

Philly and I excitedly relayed all our astounding escapades. We told him about the electric eel and skeleton swordsmen, Mad Dog, Thrak and the potty Potentate. He was amazed, and when we showed him the three beautiful treasures we had collected, his glasses steamed up in excitement!

'Ooo-eee! They are magnificent,' he cried. 'I'm sure I can utilize these in one of my miraculous machines!'

'But they're priceless, Grandpa!' complained Philly, and Jakeman gave her a wink. 'Oh Grandpa! You are a tease,' she said.

'Well, it's wonderful to have you back; both of you,' said the old man, giving his granddaughter another hug and shaking me heartily by the hand. 'Well done, Philly and well done, Charlie Small. And at long last, *welcome* to Jakeman's Works. Now, who's for some grub?'

'You bet,' I cried.

All's Well That Ends Well!

Now I'm lying in bed on the top floor of Jakeman's factory, writing up my journal. Machine parts and empty oil drums surround me; there's a strong smell of axle grease in the air; all the windows are dirty and the bed sheets look as if they've been used to clean a motorbike. But I don't mind – I don't mind one bit, because now I'm here I know I'm that much closer to getting home.

When we had finished swapping stories with Jakeman, we sat down at one of his workbenches to a wonderful meal of fish and chips, eaten with our fingers from newspaper wrapping. Nothing has ever tasted so good! Then the old inventor got out a series of drawings from a plan chest and spread them out on the bench.

'This is what's going to get you home, Charlie,' he said, pointing to the plans that looked like nothing more than a confusion of pencil lines and crossed-out calculations.

'Really?' I asked sceptically. 'What on earth is it?'

'Well, it's a sort of transporter,' beamed Jakeman. 'Er, a bit like a cross between a cannon and a . . . a . . . well, a bit like a cannon, really!'

'A cannon!' I cried. 'You're going to fire me from a cannon?'

Was Jakeman really thinking of firing Me from a cannon?

'Oh, it's a bit more sophisticated than that, Charlie,' objected Jakeman, looking a little hurt. 'A little bit more sophisticated, anyway. Let me explain . . .'

Jakeman tried to show me how his machine would catapult me back into my own time zone, but after a while even he got confused and we decided to leave it until the morning! Now I've finished bringing my journal up to date and am ready for sleep.

Hello, what's that noise? There's some sort of commotion on the stairs. I can hear a familiar-sounding voice. Who on earth is it?

'Charlie Small . . . Charlie Small? Where are you, Charlie Small?'

Oh no! It sounds like Captain Cut-throat. It can't be! What's she doing here? She should be on her way to Mayazapan with the avaricious Aveline!

'Come on, there's no use in 'iding, lad. Where are those gorgeous gewgaws you've collected? I want them for me treasure 'oard. What's more, it's about time you resumed your duties, you desertin' dog. Come on, where are you 'iding?'

CRASH! BANG!

The door to my room has burst open with a mighty crash . . . OH CRUMBS!

PUBLISHER'S NOTE

This is where Charlie's seventh journal ends. If you have any information about him, please let us know at: **www.charliesmall.co.uk**

Captain
Cut-throat is
coming
through
the
door

What
will

Boris the Chimp guard

.happen

Next?

Into the mincing machi
with them.
The Potty Potentate!
Beware, bewar
of the dreaded smoke demon

Ooh! I'm so exhausted, Charlie
Tristram Twitch the twit!
Never underestimate a giant oyster – they are lethal